"See anything you like, Lieutenant?"

Mike McDevin could only stare. Her name, she said, was Linda. Her figure, he could see for himself, was perfect. The rest was a mystery. "Is this your first leave, Lieutenant?" McDevin nodded at her.

Suddenly she was across the room and in his arms. "Welcome to London, darling," she whispered.

Two nights later McDevin had to bail out of a plane on a mission over Belgium. There he met a beautiful blonde. "Is this your first visit here, Lieutenant?" she asked. McDevin nodded, and watched her walk into his arms, her mouth ready for his kiss.

This, thought Mike McDevin, is some war!

C. L. McDERMOTT

A YANK

on Piccadilly

WILDSIDE PRESS

INTRODUCTION

D URING World War II, in the year 1944, I was one of the thousands of replacements sent to the Eighth Air Force to relieve battle-weary veterans who, having won the ETO air war, finally controlled the European skies. The German *Luftwaffe* continued to muster an uncomfortable array of fighter aircraft to bother the allied airmen, but still three divisions of B-17's and B-24's stationed throughout England rolled up an impressive record of bomb destruction on Jerry's strategic targets.

In this gory business of aerial depredation, I was a bombardier-navigator on a B-17 bomber crew. My job as a professional annihilator being odious, to say the least, I was constrained to obtain what mental relief I could by observation of my fellow Americans, suffering through the same fears and dangers as was I. It happens that I am singularly fascinated by people; and the antics of my own kind, away from home, free of family and community restrictions and motivated by a phony justification called "combat," left an impression indelibly etched within me, which has since cried out to be disseminated.

Before I continue, let me assure you that I am neither criticizing nor upholding the type of behavior which I have written about in *A Yank on Piccadilly*. Rather, I serve here in the capacity of reporter. I am not apologizing because *A Yank on Piccadilly* is admittedly risqué and naughty, even though most of my writings are tediously respectable, about prosaic things not ordinarily appealing, except in certain professional fields.

If you wonder why I wrote the book, it was a matter of simple geography. When I had leave to be away from my unit, I saw all the things in London that the usual tourist sees—Westminster Abbey, Buckingham Palace, Hyde Park, Madame Tussaud's, the British Museum, and the Tower of London. I found them all interesting, but it was when I visited Piccadilly Circus that I vowed to write this book.

Again you may ask why. Because Piccadilly Circus in wartime was the only place I had ever known which exemplified such complete, universal lack of restraint, in which so many people so openly and frankly pursued the same libertine objectives. They were human beings with the veneer of convention rubbed off— or perhaps with a different veneer added, an emotional protective coloring against the compulsions of a nerve-riddling war. I resolved that the book I was to write would be stenographic, with nothing left out, and entirely authentic. Such fiction as exists is brought in only to tie the story together—rest assured that if the incidents described did not happen to me, they did surround the lives of people whom I knew.

I had a lot of fun writing *A Yank on Piccadilly*, and I hope sincerely that you have a lot of fun reading it. If it embarrasses you, I am sorry, but before you write me a cutting reprimand, keep in mind that the book is a faithful report of things that really happened, not about *my* friends specifically, but about a large group of Americans away from home, who could easily be among *your* acquaintances or even your close friends. This is a representative story about human beings. Enjoy it!

C. L. M.

CHAPTER

1

O FFICERS' CALL WILL BE HELD ON PROMENADE DECK AFT, immediately. Repeat: Officers' Call will be held on promenade deck aft, immediately." The ship's address system growled in a cold monotone. Lieutenant Michael Patrick McDevin leaned against the ship's railing, watched some gulls tussle over a bit of galley garbage, and wondered where in hell promenade deck was. He wished that damned address system would "throw a rod," or whatever address systems do. All the way across the Irish Sea it howled and moaned.

"Officers' Call will . . ." it groaned on.

"All right! All right! I'm coming! Hold your water." But he didn't move. His eyes wandered from the gulls to the gray, dismal, Liverpool waterfront. He watched an old, drab-looking individual shielding a match from the wind as he tried to light his pipe.

"Hey, Mike!" someone piped. He didn't have to look to know it was Dick Crolley, his cockey little navigator, calling.

"Come, come, McDevin, my sex-mad brother," mocked Crolley, with his usual ingratiating grin. "Speedst thy dragging buttocks to yon milling mob."

"What is it this time?" asked McDevin as he fell in beside his navigator. "Boat drill, short-arm, or another venereal disease lecture?"

"Don't be churlish, Lieutenant; don't forget you are a member of a fighting team! 'Off we go into the wild blue yonder. . . .' " mocked Crolley.

"Dry up, will you? Give me the poop. You seem to know everything."

"Not quite everything. Some paddle-foot colonel is going to brief us and give us a welcome to 'Merrie Ole.' You know . . . 'We've got a job to do, boys. Be careful what you talk about for the enemy is listening. And the best thing to do is stay away from it, but if you can't, be careful.' The same old patter."

As they rounded the deck someone called attention for a Transportation Corps colonel who began to pour out his heart to the boys in welcome—and then began: "We have a job to do. . . ." McDevin looked around him. There were nearly two hundred pilots, navigators, and bombardiers, most of them wearing leather jackets and beaten-up, forest-green service caps. He wondered what these guys were thinking about. Home? The battle they were about to fight? Hell! He shrugged his shoulders. These immoral jackasses! The Old Man had better forget about turning these wolves loose on the dock—there wouldn't be a virgin left in Liverpool.

He laughed aloud.

"What's so damned funny?" whispered Crolley.

"I was just wondering," chortled McDevin, "if that old bastard has any sex life."

"If he does, it would be damned uninteresting compared with yours."

"True, I lead a carnal existence," admitted McDevin. "I'm a slave to desire; you're just jealous."

"Jealous? Why should I be jealous? I have no desire so I don't indulge," said Crolley with a twinkle.

"Don't indulge," sniggered McDevin. "Who in hell are you trying to fool? If I remember correctly, one night on the green at the Ardmore Country Club. . . ."

"Must we always carry on such a crude conversation? My mind is much too delicate to be subjected to such fiddle-faddle."

The colonel by this time was well into the importance of conservation in communications and combat zones. . . . "A crust of bread must not go uneaten, et cetera."

"I'm sweating this old fossil out," remarked Bill Canyon, pilot and strong man of the crew. "Guys like this can ruin my whole day."

"Aside from the fact it will be a cold day in hell when you stay awake long enough to know the difference between night and day," said Crolley, in sweet sarcasm, "might I ask who pulled your chain?"

"Are you two fishmongers at it again?" continued Canyon, completely unabashed. "You two gab more and say less than any two old women I know."

"Don't be a boor, my dear Canyon. The lieutenant and I were discussing ethics in our postwar chosen profession, pimping and fopping. 'In the satisfaction of the senses lies the greatest and highest good,' " said McDevin dramatically.

With a flourish of his swagger stick and jackanapish flick at his grommeted, fur-felt service cap the colonel sniffed and strode away with his toad-eating, tuft-hunting staff scurrying in his wake, each with his vial of rose water, each laying the flattering unction to the colonel's soul. Gilding the pill, so to speak.

"And now," said Canyon, breaking the silence, "the latrine awaits your pleasure, gentlemen. May I suggest a three-way tête-à-tête?"

Three hours later five hundred officers and enlisted men descended the gangplank of the *Penguin* to touch English soil, and cause joy in the hearts of English lasses, and pungent passion in the hearts of English thane and noble alike.

They marched "route step" (and indeed do flyers march any other way?) the short distance through the streets of Liverpool from the docks to the railroad station. Those natives who were on the street stopped to give the V-for-victory sign, or just to watch, coldly and with reserve. A few of the girls waved, and the Yanks already stationed there smiled and with a wise look remarked, "You won't like it here."

A red-faced Bobby stopped along his beat to view again a familiar sight and to listen to familiar Yankee wisecracks. "Look at the head on that one." But he had heard that before when another group of replacements landed in Liverpool and marched from the docks to the railroad station.

McDevin looked at the dreary city. It hadn't been entirely untouched by the German blitz of 1939. There was a bombed-out building here and there, and gnarled and twisted metal. The people were kind of queer-looking ducks, he thought. All dressed so uninterestingly—and looked as if they couldn't smile. They stood there like so many icebergs; as if they had found a home in their reticence. Jesus, what a cheerless hole!

He nudged Crolley who was marching beside him. "Cast your peepers at that nice ripe tomato about eleven o'clock. How would you like to try that for size?"

"Now look at her face," replied his navigator.

"Not bad when you compare her with these other spooks."

"Come now, McDevin, you can do better than that. Gaze at what's coming in about one-thirty."

9

"Well, *well!*" exclaimed Michael Patrick in genuine appreciation. "Donuts!"

"And look what's carrying them. An honest-to-God, unadulterated, beautiful American Red Cross girl," drooled Crolley.

"Did someone mention adultery?" asked Bill Canyon, who was directly behind them.

"Raise your mind to stomach level and gaze with envy and awe, my boy," suggested McDevin, "for here is a lesson to remember. You, with the fire and vitality of youth, enlisted to fight in the skies, to deal death and destruction to those that threaten world security and peace. You volunteered that you might have an opportunity to protect your sisters and mother from the ravages of a heartless enemy. And now you are about to embark on twenty-five butt-risking missions while some gravel-agitating paddle-foot sits in Liverpool for the duration, playing night-games with this lovely hunk of female."

"Donut, boys?" smiled the beauty.

"Why, yes, thank you," croaked Canyon.

"Take two, they're small," chimed McDevin.

"Tell me, dear," asked Crolley complacently. "Are there any more at home like you?"

"Here we go again," sighed the lovely. "I'm an only child. I'm not in the market for boy friends. I come from Puerto Rico and I know you don't. I've been in England for four months and, yes, I'm anxious to get home. I've read a book, I bowl a sweet one seventy when I'm in the States, and I sleep with my beard outside the covers. Is there anything else you would like to know?"

"Yeah. Whose beard?" grinned McDevin. "Don't mind my gruesome friend here. He's wanted by every wolf-hunter in Ohio."

"And I suppose you're not?" taunted the girl. "Look, fellows, I have to put up with this every time replacements come through. I'm a married woman and my husband is adjutant to the Port Commander. 'Bye." And she swirled away, her powder-blue uniform contrasting beautifully with the forest green and olive drab.

"Snippy little wench," observed McDevin. "They're all alike."

Just then an angry little train scampered toward them and came to an indignant stop immediately abreast of the group.

"Looks like a two-bit ride in Coney Island, doesn't it?" scoffed Crolley.

"How would you know?" asked McDevin. "The farthest away from Springfield you ever were was Columbus until the Army gave you a free ride to the Republic of Texas."

"You do the boy an injustice," interposed Bill Canyon. "His old man was a barker in a Coney Island bottle show during Prohibition."

"Silence, you peasants. When you mention the name Springfield, you will also mention Ohio, and how your head in deepest reverence. Furthermore, it may interest you to know my old man rules Springfield's Plum Street with nothing but an iron hand."

Someone with authority had given the order to board the train, such as it was, and everyone scrambled madly for seats. McDevin and Crolley followed big Bill Canyon's interference and the three of them were soon ensconced in a compartment. The train moved out in the opposite direction from which it had come.

The two-hour ride was slow and more or less uneventful. The three inseparables observed their usual garrulity with McDevin and Crolley the butts of each other's travesties. Now and then Canyon introduced a remark only to be immediately set upon by the combined forces of his two burlesquing pals.

At their destination they were met by a pale, gray-haired, pseudo-tough captain who led them the quarter-mile to the Replacement Depot so fondly remembered by Eighth and Ninth Air Force personnel as Stone. It was growing dusk and the company streets were empty. The dampness and apparent emptiness gave rise to unpleasant associations, and McDevin shivered.

"Holy Christ, this place is a thanatopsis," he said, looking about.

"Only about this time of day, or when the sun doesn't shine," returned the captain, who had assumed charge at the station. "It looks rather gloomy now, but tomorrow morning you won't even remember it."

"Do we get a chance to go to town—that is, if there's one in the vicinity?" Crolley wanted to know.

"It will take a couple of days for you to process. After that the Old Man will give you a VOCO from 1600 to 2400 every day. There's a town called Stoke-on-Trent about ten or twelve miles from here. Cabbies come to the gate every afternoon and for ten shillings they'll take you in."

"I can see right now all we can depend on are 'quickies.' Hell, it's ten o'clock now and it's just getting dark. That's kind of rushing things. You'll only get an hour of darkness to work in before you'll have to start back to the base," moaned Crolley.

"By Gawd!" declared the captain. "Is that all you guys think of? Damned if I don't believe some of you young bloods wouldn't crawl a mile on your bellies just to look at a woman through a chicken-wire fence."

"What a disgustingly brutal way to put it," mocked Crolley.

"Don't you realize we're at war and it's too serious to be fooled around with? You youngsters can't seem to realize what we're up against."

"It's especially dangerous for you, isn't it, Captain?" said Bill Canyon with derision. "It must be tough to have to march these combat officers and men back and forth between the railroad station and the base. Why a truck or jeep might come along any day and set you right on your backside."

"Say, Lieutenant, just to whom do you think you're talking?"

"I'm talking to an old coot who as a civilian probably was a butcher or a clerk in a laundry and who now holds the rank of captain trying to be tough. Listen, chum, there are officers in this outfit who have had more time at attention than you've had in the Army."

The captain halted the group.

"Lieutenant, I'm not about to take anything from an insolent young puppy like you. I'll have your ass nailed to my bedroom door for what you just said."

"You won't have mine or anybody's else's ass on your door. These combat groups are being hit so hard they're crying for replacements. You stop me from going with my crew and your ass will be nailed to *my* door."

"I order you to report to my office tomorrow morning at nine o'clock. You'll find it in headquarters—my name is Captain Jack R. Logan."

A silence had fallen over the entire group.

The captain continued: "Now all of you go into this building

12

here and take a seat. We'll be with you in a short while to give you your instructions."

There was a moment of silence, then Crolley said in a voice that smacked of a women's club program-committee chairman at an afternoon tea, "And now, Captain Jack will favor us with 'The Air Corps Song.' "

The next two days were spent processing and censoring enlisted men's mail. During the evening English "mild and bitter" took its toll.

The first night McDevin and Crolley eagerly awaited the opening of the bar in the Officers' Club. The "mild and bitter" was served typically in pint mugs and the two began with four apiece, "just for laughs" as Crolley put it. The first draught was commented upon caustically by the pair, but resigning themselves to it as a necessary nuisance, they consumed large quantities.

"This stuff," remarked Crolley, "if it were sold in Ohio, would be given its proper name and served directly from the horse."

After the sixteenth mug had been emptied they were led to their quarters by big Bill Canyon, who was a total abstainer for sometimes a week at a time. A catastrophe was barely averted when Crolley began systematically to awaken each sleeper in the barracks informing him the world had suddenly become alight with fire and each was under moral obligation to rise to the occasion and extinguish the blaze in the proper and accepted manner.

It was the twenty-fifth of July when Mc Devin and his companions found themselves in a combat bombardment group. There had been GI trucks at the little station and now everyone had lined up by crews on the ramp. Some lieutenant colonel was calling crew members and making squadron assignments.

"Crew one-two-five, Lieutenant William R. Canyon, Pilot, 838th."

"And now what?" whispered Crolley. "Are they going to line us up and throw rocks? I don't like it here."

"Can't say I'm in love with the place myself," retorted McDevin.

"Yeah. Grab a gander at that Seventeen sitting over there. Why that sonovabitch has more holes than Canyon's head."

"A masterpiece of understatement," announced McDevin.

"Yeah, I know, but the Seventeen had guns to protect itself."

The colonel had begun to speak. "Gentlemen, may I extend you a welcome because it's the only one you're going to get. This is your new home and you probably won't like it one damned bit."

"What an altruistic soul—nothing but cheer," soliloquized McDevin.

"Now get on these trucks and they'll take you to your respective squadrons. We have a mission coming in in about twenty minutes and you can meet the boys—what's left of them. Now, are there any questions?"

"Yeah. When's sick call?" called Crolley.

"There's one in every crowd," sighed the colonel. "Now for the information of those of you who are not quite so wise, you'll probably fly your first mission in about ten days, unless, of course, the Jerries have a field day in the meantime. The pilot will ride co-pilot with an experienced crew on one mission before we'll trust him with a ship of his own and an inexperienced crew. Those among you who show any signs of intelligence will be assigned to lead—your only reward for that will be top

14

billing on Papa Goering's black list. Forty-eight-hour passes will be issued by crews in turn as long as there are enough men available to cover a mission. Now get on these trucks and ask your questions when you get to your squadron area. We gotta clear this ramp." His tone was lifeless and he sounded very, very tired.

There was a scramble and the trucks headed for their respective squadron areas, traveling down the left side of the road.

"Hey," complained Corporal "Porky" Terrian, ball-turret gunner of the crew. "These dumb bastards are on the wrong side of the road."

"Christ, you're stupid," informed the radio operator, Sergeant Gordon Goud. "Any goddamned fool knows it's customary to drive on the wrong side of the road in the Army. Don't they teach you nothing in Massachusetts?"

The GI truck growled indignantly, slackened speed, and spat contemptuously; McDevin and his companions viewed with anticipation the 838th Squadron Area which was the first scene set for the "acts" to come.

The area was composed of eighteen or nineteen Nissen huts, placed in no particular order. They were olive drab in color and appeared to be large tubes that had been halved latitudinally and plugged at each end. The orderly room, a square, concrete, dismal-looking building, was set away from the others. Just outside its doorway stood a short, disgruntled-looking first lieutenant, and a gnarled first sergeant who looked as if he had done everything there was to do twice and hadn't liked it either time. The lieutenant spoke with conviction.

"It's about time they sent us replacements. Christ, we're so short of men with all these crews going down I can't even get a decent latrine detail."

"Oh, oh," whispered Terrian. "This guy and me ain't gonna be buddies at all. It's guys like him what ruins things for guys like me."

"What can you expect?" reminded Goud. "He's a gravel agitator. They're always eager. Don't worry, Canyon will get us out of any details."

"Oh, yeah?" sneered Terrian. "Don't look now, but that miscarriage with the six stripes on his sleeve is pointin' right at you an' Lieutenant Canyon ain't doin' nothin' but havin' an argu-

15

ment with Lieutenant McDevin. He ain't even lookin' this way."

"Hey, you!" roared the miscarriage. "All I want to see is ass and elbows! Get on that baggage detail! An' don't gimme any of your lip or I'll have you runnin' that ramp till you ain't got nothin' but bloody stumps for legs!"

The little lieutenant, whose name was Whitsong, was a worn-out guy with a mustache. He was the administrative officer for the squadron and a worrier of the first water. He was convinced the entire world had concentrated its powers for the sole purpose of causing discomfort, confusion, and embarrassment for Lieutenant Whitsong. He was attempting to appear nonchalant and at ease to McDevin and Crolley, but he spoke wearily as if he were under a great strain.

"You officers on Canyon's crew can sleep in Hut Thirteen and you can assign your enlisted men to number twenty-seven. Supply is right over there across from the mailroom—you can draw a couple of blankets there. Oh, yeah, and forty-fives, too. Jesus, I'm glad to see you fellows. There ain't anybody left any more. Seems like every time they fly a mission they lose sixty per cent. The club is up this road about a quarter of a mile. They got the goddamnedest whiskey up there you ever tasted. If you want to know anything just drop around to the orderly room."

Crolley told the enlisted men which hut they were to occupy and joined McDevin and Canyon who had begun to hunt number thirteen. They found it near the edge of the area, next to a pasture which had a pond in the middle. They hesitated before opening the door. As usual, Crolley broke the silence:

"Here, gentlemen, is the buy of a lifetime. Only twelve thousand dollars for this little palace—a bargain that you'll find no other place in Merrie Old England. What a beautiful location for a whorehouse. Why you'll make yourselves rich before you know it. With all these males about you can't miss. . . ."

"Shut up and open the door," ordered McDevin good naturedly.

"A thousand pardons, sire," begged Crolley, as he bowed elaborately and swept the ground with his cap.

Number thirteen was one of the few huts in the entire group which was divided in halves. Each half had four beds, a small stove, and two dressers. There was brown linoleum on the floor

16

and an electric light hung from the center of the ceiling. On each bed were three English "biscuits" laid end to end. A coal pail and shovel stood by the stove and there were blackout curtains of thick, velvety material hanging on each of the two windows. Someone had attempted to paint the walls and ceiling, but with little success.

"What?" exclaimed Crolley with pretended disdain. "No paramours?"

"And no swimming pool?" added McDevin. "Ah, but yes, gentlemen, there is a war on and each of us must give up some little thing. We must be guided by the ancient adage, 'Don't cry because you have no shoes; today I saw a man who had no feet.' "

"Which all goes to show you," declaimed Crolley, "them which has, gits."

"May I suggest," said McDevin, "that Lieutenant Crolley and myself place our escutcheons on the sacks nearest the stove and allow Lieutenant Canyon the special advantage of a pad next to the window where he may enjoy the full benefits of the wintry blasts. All in favor say *aye*."

"Aye," voted Crolley and McDevin simultaneously, and they dived for their chosen beds.

"Hey," objected Canyon. "You guys are always screwing me. Let's draw straws."

"Come now," scolded Crolley. "Would you stoop so low as a game of chance? *Tsk, tsk*. For shame. And when McDevin and I were just about to declare you Grand High Potentate and Supreme Cotquean, Local Number 13. Where's your gratitude, man, your sense of decency?"

"Sometimes you birds give me a pain," complained Canyon.

"Why, Bill, you hurt us to the quick," reproached McDevin. "Do you actually believe Dick and I would try to beat you out of anything? We're just trying to do you a favor."

"Okay, okay," groaned Canyon, "but someday I'm going to throw both you bastards out the bomb bay."

"And now threats." Crolley shook his head sadly and winked at McDevin.

The trio located supply and a sergeant issued each one, with a marked lack of enthusiasm, two blankets, a caliber forty-five automatic and holster, a gas mask and a steel flak helmet. McDevin's helmet was leather-covered, smaller and more closely fitting than the others to enable him better to "engage" the bombsight.

"Don't you wish you were a bombardier? This helmet is the latest out. Everybody is raving about it," quipped McDevin.

A baggage truck had arrived, and while McDevin and his two companions were unpacking, two captains entered number thirteen.

"Anybody here from Chicago?" asked one.

"Ohio, Iowa and Wyoming," answered McDevin.

"I'm Doc Lerdner and this is Misch Hour. He's squadron navigator and I'm the flight surgeon."

"Glad to know you. My name's McDevin, Mike McDevin; this is Dick Crolley, and the ape in the corner is Bill Canyon."

Everybody shook hands.

"We live in the other half of the hut so we thought we'd drop over and welcome you to the 838th. Thought maybe we could help you out. Say, where's your co-pilot? We need co-pilots bad," said Hour seriously.

"We left him in a hospital in Nutt's Corner, Ireland," informed Crolley, "but it's just as well; he wasn't worth a good goddamn."

Captain Hour was middle-sized and had a Roman-type nose and an almost beet-red face that smiled all over when he spoke. His head was small and crowned by a hank of straight, blond hair. He was one of the most popular men in the squadron and the most capable and dependable all around officer in the entire group.

Everybody liked Doc Lerdner, a large, raw-boned individual with high cheekbones and a broad forehead. His hands were large and appeared to be as resilient as rubber. In civilian life he had been one of Chicago's foremost obstetricians. He breathed as though his throat were choked with phlegm.

Hour swallowed. "By the way, you didn't bring any American bourbon, did you? I'll trade you two quarts of rotgut Scotch for a quart of anything made in the U. S. A."

"We brought six or seven fifths of stuff," said Crolley, "but we don't want to trade. We're saving them for Christmas."

"Christmas!" exclaimed Doc Lerdner with surprise. "Why, hell, that's months away. You don't expect to be alive—I mean, well, Christ, that's a long time to wait."

There was a silence. Doc looked embarrassed and Hour laughed halfheartedly.

"What the Doc really means is maybe you'll be on your way home or the war will be over or—or something," observed Hour irresolutely.

"Yeah," apologized Doc. "Don't pay any attention to me."

"You win. Let's break that bottle of Taylor you stole from the Officers' Club in Kearney, Dick," proposed McDevin. "You don't want that on your conscience, do you?"

"May I suggest," countered Crolley, "we crack that Grandad you copped from the strip-teaser in the carnival in Ardmore? What an archfield! He gets this tomato drunk on her own booze; screws hell out of her; then, when she passes out, walks away with a bottle of her best liquor."

"These two thieves will be arguing all night. I brought an extra bottle for just such an occasion," smiled Canyon. "Here's a fifth of something and I'll open it on condition we kill it here and now. Any objections?"

"The first man who opens his mouth gets my foot in it," warned Hour.

"So! Been holding out on your old buddies, huh?" snorted Crolley. "You brought an extra bottle. A fine pilot you turned out to be, you Gila monster, you. Can't even trust you to tell us when you got booze. How do you expect us to trust you in the air?"

"Now, now, Crolley," soothed Doc Lerdner. "Maybe he thought it was for the best."

"Man, oh, man, it never fails," sighed McDevin. "We were drunk when we reached Ardmore. We got drunk as soon as we hit Kearney. Ditto at Bangor. We stayed drunk for four days during the interim at Gander Field. We got crocked as loons at Stone, and now that we have arrived in the Group, before we even have chow or make our sacks, we start in on a fifth of VO, just for the hell of it. We're going to end up dipsomaniacs, for sure."

"I know of only one better way to die," said Hour.

"Ah, I see we have another concupiscent soul among us," said Crolley.

"Okay, Bill, if we're going to drink it, let's get at it. And get that goddamned grin off your puss. Just 'cause you pulled a fast

19

one for a change, isn't a sign you have any brains," said Mc-Devin impatiently.

"Oh, yes. I nearly forgot. Just by chance I have some glasses over in the hut. I'll go get a few," remarked Doc.

"Just by chance, your ass, Doc, but go get 'em anyway," said Crolley.

The fifth was just enough to taste like more. At five o'clock the quintet wended its way the quarter-mile to officers' mess. Hour and Lerdner saw to it that everyone in the 838th became acquainted with the new crew and to drop a subtle hint that six or seven fifths of American bourbon had also arrived in the Group.

"Well, welcome, friends, welcome to our little organization," boomed big Willie Birtland, a happy, round-faced bombardier from Dallas. "Now I tell you what I'm going to do for you fellows. I'm going to let you give me your bourbon for safe-keeping. With all these sticky-fingered Yankees around here, it isn't safe to keep anything so valuable as American bourbon unless you know the ropes. . . ."

"Glad to know you, Birtland," interrupted Crolley. "Let's go into the bar and line up some rotgut and leave the good stuff until later."

They walked into the lounge part of the officers' mess and went directly to the bar, an affair about twenty feet in length, situated at the far end of the building. Drinks, rotten as they were, were served by a couple of GI's by the names of Jimmie and Murph. Jimmie, from the Eastside, nobody knew of what, was a professional bartender and had used his ingenuity to make the bar "authentic" down to the footrail. Scotch and gin were available but nobody knew the difference after a few drinks. From seven-thirty on, Jimmie and Murph poured indiscriminately from whichever bottle was nearer.

McDevin noticed that no one appeared either glad or sorry to meet the new replacements. However, it was easy to differentiate between the old and the new. It was nothing he could put his finger on, but it was undeniably there.

As they ordered the second round of drinks, Willie Birtland announced, "Here I go again. I've had it."

"You're a damned fool if you haven't," remarked Crolley, casually.

"Absolutely correct, Crolley. I think no home should be without it," agreed McDevin.

"I forgot you guys are new," apologized Birtland. " 'You've had it' or 'I've had it' or 'he's had it' are phrases we picked up from the limeys. It means . . . well, it means . . . you've had it."

"Very enlightening. You express yourself beautifully and with decision," said McDevin.

"For Christ's sake, do you want me to draw you a picture?"

"Never mind," said McDevin. "I believe the enigma will somehow unveil itself."

At eleven o'clock the bar closed and the club began to empty. Back in number thirteen the three began to prepare for bed.

"Did you notice those guys tonight?" asked Crolley. "They all acted like they didn't give a damn about anything. And a lot of them looked scared, in a way."

"My achin' back," complained McDevin. "Is this going to be another one of your dirges?"

"No, not exactly. I was just thinking."

"This is a hell of a time to do that."

"You know, we three are a dirty lot of bastards. We've committed every sin in the Book except murder and incest. This combat flying could very well be a Nemesis in itself."

"Don't be unwholesome. Sometimes you remind me of a dirty old man."

"What's a Nemesis?" asked Canyon, as he extinguished the light. "And shut up, will ya, so I can get some sack time."

"Did you hear anything, Mike?" asked Crolley.

"Nothing of importance," answered McDevin.

"They tell me Bill Canyon was the best in Waterloo. All of the boys were crazy over him," chided Crolley.

And the battle lasted well into the night.

CHAPTER

3

THE TRAINING OFFICER OF THE 838TH SQUADRON WASTED NO time. The next morning at nine the new crews sat in the training block listening to lectures and studying the combat gear they would use. There was a number of mock-ups, demonstrating the workings of various pieces of equipment.

"Spencer was right," muttered Crolley.

"Who was Spencer?" asked Canyon.

"A joker who had some damned sound ideas. He held that the universe has evolved from relative simplicity to relative complexity through mechanical forces," answered Crolley.

Canyon snorted.

"Go ahead and snort. If it weren't for mechanical forces, we wouldn't be about to have blood on our lily-white hands. We would be happy to sit about and gnaw bones and eat raw meat and drag a woman around by her hair all day. The only piece of machinery I condone is a distillery."

"Sometimes I think you're out of your head," said Canyon impatiently. "Why don't you listen to what the man says? Maybe you might learn something you can use later."

"Go join a union and maybe they'll give you a box to preach from. Don't you have any imagination?"

During the course of the day they were introduced to sundry items born of war to which they had hitherto been strangers. Of greatest interest, however, especially to Crolley, were "flak suits." They were cumbersome affairs, composed of overlapping pieces of metal covered with khaki-colored cloth. They were biblike in appearance and augmented by an apron which covered the abdomen and pubic region. Because of the vulnerability of his position, the bombardier was given extra consideration. His apron was of a special variety. It extended well back under his crotch.

"You see, gentlemen, it pays to be a bombardier," exclaimed McDevin to Canyon and Crolley. "When this war is over I can go home with my prize possessions intact and in operational order, while you peasants greet American womanhood with nothing but memories."

The day passed uneventfully as did the several days which followed. McDevin and his companions were being prepared to fly combat.

Despite a seven-day-a-week, twenty-four-hour-a-day availability, even a combat group can find time for recreation. So it happened that six nights after the arrival of McDevin and his crew the Group sponsored a magnificent party.

The Officers' Club was transformed into a virtual Bacchic tabernacle. Makeshift bars were placed at every turning. A truckload of Scotch was hauled in from London.

GI transportation was dispatched to Bury St. Edmunds, Cambridge, and London to bring girls of varied descriptions and creeds. An orchestra composed of enlisted men provided strictly American rhythm and jive from seven-thirty until the liquor supply was completely exhausted.

The mess sergeant, Sergeant Berg, outdid himself in food preparations, although no expert was needed to discern the "Army touch."

The bars were opened at five o'clock and McDevin, Crolley and Canyon were among the early arrivals. Crolley, the mathematician of the trio, laid down his strategy for the evening.

"Now, this is the way I've got it doped out: ten pounds apiece will carry us until about one-thirty in the morning. That's about forty bucks, which isn't so bad for an evening's entertainment."

"How do you figure?" asked Canyon.

"Well, a double shot costs two shillings sixpence mixed. On an average we ought to knock off a drink every fifteen minutes. That's eight ounces an hour. There are roughly thirty ounces in a quart, and to preserve our self-respect we should polish off a couple of quarts apiece. So, taking an hour out for chow, two quarts per head will last us until about one-thirty. Two quarts at two and six per double shot will cost about seven pounds ten shillings. That will leave about two pounds ten to spend on the broads."

"Which is too goddamned much," declared Canyon.

"Why the scientific approach? That's a hell of a way to begin a party," interposed McDevin. "And I suppose before you pass out we'll have to listen to a statistical resumé of the evening's

23

monetary expenditures. Next you'll be telling us how many ergs of energy we'll need to last the night. Why the devil can't you just drink and play with the tomatoes and let it go at that?"

"That would be the easy way, Mike," laughed Crolley.

Just then a group of girls walked in the door of the bar amid the moans and sex-manifested growls and whistles of the roomful of America's "cream of the crop."

"Shut up and prepare for action," McDevin snapped.

"Look at the tall job with the sleepy eyes and the little brunette with her," said Crolley.

"Okay, Shorty. Slim one's mine. You take the runt. And for Gawd's sake, let's hope Canyon stays out of the hut," returned Mike and started for the game.

"What d'ya mean . . ." protested Bill, but McDevin and Crolley were gone.

The tall girl with sleepy eyes looked more than her twenty-four years. She wore her hair close to her head and her eyebrows were carefully arched. She looked around disdainfully and smoothed her skirt around well-proportioned hips. Hoseless legs rose gracefully from well-turned ankles and her small, neatly shod feet moved daintily across the floor. McDevin made a pass from twelve o'clock high.

"How do you do, Miss," crooned Mike. "Permit me to introduce myself. I'm Lieutenant Mike McDevin and this is Lieutenant Dick Crolley."

"Good evening, Lieutenant." Her voice was low and rich. "My name is Linda Chambers and this is Doris Errington. Good night." And she moved away.

McDevin was by her side quickly, and Crolley followed the brunette.

"We thought perhaps you would like to let us escort you for the evening," offered Mike.

"We can do quite well left to our own devices, thank you, Lieutenant," Linda said coldly.

"You came here to dance, didn't you?" asked Crolley.

"Yes," retorted Doris, "but not to be set upon by American wolves." But her deep brown eyes were soft and yielding and betrayed her.

"Well, won't you have a drink and we can talk it over," begged McDevin. "Dinner will be served soon and of course you'll want someone to take you. Besides, I know the mess sergeant and he's got some steaks he appropriated from the colonel's kitchen."

"Steaks? I would so like a steak, Linda. Let's give it a try," ventured Doris Errington. "They can't be any worse than the others."

Linda tried hard to give the impression of doubt, but after a proper amount of protest she agreed.

"No funny business," she warned, with just the slightest mischief in her blue eyes.

There were two makeshift bars near the rear of the room and McDevin and Crolley led their quarry to the more remote of the two.

"What will you drink? Scotch or gin-and-orange?" asked Mike politely.

"Scotch, of course. For the both of us, if you please," and her tone was noticeably warmer.

McDevin slipped a ten shilling note to the GI bartender and muttered, "These bitches have to leave around eleven o'clock. Make those drinks stiff."

"Gotcha," whispered the bartender knowingly. "Good luck. There are some bunks still set up over in the big room in the annex. Some crews from the 93rd were weathered in here last night."

"Thanks, buddy," replied McDevin gratefully. Then he said in a louder voice, so that the girls and Crolley could hear, "Give us four scotch-and-sodas from the special case we flew in from Glasgow."

With drinks in hand the four found a table and waited for dinner.

"Have you been here before?" asked Crolley, starting the conversation.

"Just once, about three months ago," answered Doris. She was plump with a pert little nose and large, innocent eyes which were in sharp contrast to the hard lines at the edge of her sensuous lips. Her hands were her most attractive single feature, with long, beautifully curved fingers. Her legs lacked the shapeliness of Linda's but her bosom was full and set off the rest of her body. "Some captain tried to lure me to his billet," she confessed; and then chortled, "The dope wanted something for nothing, but he was fooled."

McDevin and Crolley exchanged glances.

"All you Americans can think of is taking a girl to bed," said Linda with a frown. "And you are so damned crude about it. If you must go to bed why can't you be a bit gentle and subtle?"

"I don't know. Why cawn't we?" said McDevin, mimicking her broad British A. "It seems to me that you're the ones who brought up this sex business. We haven't said a word about it, and so far as I can see we haven't done a thing out of the way."

"Hell!" snapped Linda, "I heard you telling the chap at the bar to make our drinks stiff. And if you think you can lure me to that annex with the bunks, you are quite mistaken, Lieutenant. If you try, I shall leave you straightway!"

"Let's dance," said Mike sheepishly. "I'm sorry. I guess I pegged you wrong."

"Pegged me?"

"Misjudged you."

The band, composed of GI's, was playing *Black Magic* and the floor was filled with swaying bodies. Some of the officers were several sheets in the wind by this time, since many of them started the party early in the evening.

McDevin was silent at first, carefully guiding Linda through the crowd.

"Suddenly you are quiet, Lieutenant," said Linda coyly.

"I'm doing penance," answered McDevin contritely. Then he added, "Call me Mike, huh?"

"I'm sorry if I was abrupt," said Linda, "but after all you were quite presuming."

"I apologize."

He pulled her gently to him and Linda laid her head against his cheek and grasped the back of his neck with her hand. Her body yielded to his arms and pressed close to him.

"You're forgiven," she whispered softly, and McDevin held her tighter.

Bill Canyon had been standing on the sidelines, watching the entire proceedings with considerable amusement. As McDevin and Linda danced by, he tapped Mike on the shoulder.

"May I cut in?"

"Beat it, Bill. I was here first. Go get your own squaw."

"Now is that any way to talk to your pilot? *Tsk, tsk!*"

"Scram, dammit!"

"Lieutenant, where are your manners? How about an introduction to the young lady?"

"Oh, for . . . Okay, robber," McDevin said with resignation. "Miss Chambers, may I introduce Lieutenant Bill Canyon, probably the most hated man in the entire United States Army."

"It's a pleasure, Miss Chambers," said Bill suavely.

"Hey, wait a minute. Where in hell did you get this charm, all of a sudden? The only guy in the group with two left feet and now you're waxing Clark Gable on me. Okay, okay! Now that you have met her, get on your horse and ride away."

"Oh, Mike," cooed Linda, "don't be so ignoble. So glad to know you Lieutenant Canyon," and she extended her hand. Canyon grinned at McDevin and with exaggerated chivalry bowed and kissed Linda's hand.

"May I have the honor of the remainder of this dance?"

"I would be delighted," bubbled Linda, and the two whirled away in the crowd as McDevin stalked back to his table. Crolley and Doris were gone.

When the dance was over, Linda and Bill strolled leisurely to the table, laughing and talking.

"I hope you die," grumbled McDevin, and then added vehemently, "tonight!"

"Lieutenant Canyon is a superb dancer, Mike. You should take lessons."

"Nuts."

Bill sat down across from McDevin and offered Linda a cigarette.

"Quite a shindig, ain't it," he remarked, lapsing back to his normal expression.

"Yeah, ain't it," muttered McDevin with sarcasm.

"I'm starved," Linda said. "Isn't dinner being served yet?"

"I believe it is," said Canyon. "Let's get started so we don't have to wait. There's a big crowd here tonight."

"Now listen, Bill, enough is enough. Get the hell out of here. Why ruin the night for both of us," sputtered Mike, losing his self-composure. "I think you've carried this joke far enough."

"Why, Mike," said Linda, "you're jealous. And we've only just met."

"I apologize, Linda, but this big ape thinks he's being funny and he's not, a damn bit. Every time Crolley and I get a couple of girls he has to stick his big Roman nose into the act. Now damn it, Bill, get the hell out of here. Go on back to the hut and read your dirty books or something."

A big grin spread over Bill's countenance. "I'll tell you what I'll do. I'm not planning to make a play for any babe tonight. I'm just going to get drunk and go home. Let's all go in and eat together and then I'll leave you and Linda alone."

"You really don't have to go, Bill," crooned Linda. "You're a much better dancer than Mike and you've been most decent to me since we met. You haven't insulted me once."

McDevin groaned.

Just then Crolley and Doris came back to the table, arm in arm.

"Dick is quite fascinating, really," gushed Doris. "Already he's asked me to the annex twice. And to top it off, his father is fabulously wealthy." They both sat down across the table.

"Wealthy, hell," said Canyon. "His old man's a pearl diver in some greasy spoon in Springfield."

"You should have been castrated as a boy," said Crolley pointedly. "If you begin to propagate the race over here, God save England." And he drained the dregs from his glass.

"Really, they must serve dinner soon, I'm simply starved," said Linda. "I say, if you know the mess sergeant, Mike, it seems to me you could get us some special service."

"I'm not moving an inch until this broad-shouldered abortion gets his sticky fingers off you and out of my life for the rest of the night."

"But his fingers aren't a bit sticky. He's really quite gentle. If you must be so jealous, can't you be jealous while we eat?"

The GI bartender tapped McDevin on the shoulder and said in a knowing voice, "Want a couple stiffies, Lootenant? I got a special drink that'll guarantee you results in half the time. If you need any equipment, I got that too."

"Have you got him trained, Mike?" asked Linda with contempt. "Immediately you walk in with a girl, he begins pouring out drinks and supplying you with all the necessary junk you need for a lay. Don't you think that's rather presumptuous? I've always known you Americans were crude, but you take the bloody cake."

"I'm sorry, Linda. I told you that I pegged you wrong, and I apologize for it. This guy's trying to be helpful."

Just then someone mentioned that dinner was served and the little group was caught in the rush toward the officers' dining room. It was a long, huge room, running parallel to the lounge, furnished with narrow tables on each side with an aisle down the middle. Halfway toward the back on the right was the kitchen, and from it poured steaming platters of spam, powdered eggs, and canned vegetables. Large GI tin trays served as plates, and black coffee was served in heavy white mugs. McDevin and Crolley, following Dick's preconceived plan, grabbed a place close to the big steam tables whence the food was dispensed. There were no chairs, only long benches hitched to the tables. Bill Canyon having had his fun, joined a group of stags across the room, leaving McDevin and Crolley to their own pursuits.

"Jesus Christ, do they call this crap food?" screamed Crolley. "My old man throws better stuff than this away!"

"Apparently you don't know the mess sergeant well, do you?" coolly inquired Doris,of McDevin.

"He just doesn't know that we're out here. If you'll wait a minute I'll see what I can do." He got up and brushed his lips lightly across Linda's forehead, squeezed her shoulders and murmured, "I'll be back in a moment, darling."

He found Sergeant Berg in the kitchen, doing things to a vast T-bone steak. McDevin approached him with, "Hi-ya, Sergeant. How's the chow situation?"

"You're new, ain'cha?" muttered the sergeant between mouthfuls. He didn't even bother to look up, for in his dominion he was king and he catered to no one.

"Look, Sergeant, we've got a couple of hot babes sitting out there and if we expect to play house with them I have to give them some decent chow. Here's a couple of pounds, do you think you could see your way clear?"

The sergeant attacked his steak with renewed vigor. "Can't hear you, Lootenant."

"Goddamn it, Sergeant, that's eight dollars and six cents in American rocks!"

"Do you want me to get in trouble, Lootenant? It's against the regulations and besides the mess officer's a hard man."

"Listen, Sergeant, if you can sit back here and eat steak so can
29

the rest of us, and when you speak to an officer stand up. Haven't you ever heard of military discipline?"

"Ain't you ever heard of the Articles of War which says you officers ain't supposed to try to bribe us poor enlisted men on account of because the President don't like it?"

"The colonel wouldn't like it if he knew you were eating his steak, Sergeant," snapped McDevin.

Sergeant Berg placidly masticated like a contented milch cow which was at peace with the world. "Look, Lootenant, every night I get the same story and no one's told the colonel yet. If you want steak, it'll cost you five pounds; if you don't want steak, eat spam; if you want to tell the colonel, go ahead. Him and me is good friends and what I don't know about him and that Red Cross girl shouldn't happen to nobody. Threats ain't gonna get you nowhere . . . us GI's got to live like anybody else. If you want a dame bad enough, and you got to have steak to get her, just give me the five pounds. That kinda makes a pimp out of me . . . kind of a assessory on account of the fact or somethin'. For five pounds I don't mind being a assessory, but I ain't goin' to take any more of your stuff. This is my kitchen and if you ain't got five pounds, get the hell out of here before I tell the mess officer." And he picked up the bone and began gnawing away the last fragments of the coveted meat.

McDevin was nonplussed and at a loss for words. "Okay, you goddamned bloodsucker, here's your five pounds. There's four of us, where do we sit?"

"Bring your bitches back here and I'll set you up a table in the storeroom. Why'n't ya bring a bottle with you and for another pound I'll bring you setups, and when you get 'em good and drunk you can make love to them on the potato sacks. They're kinda lumpy, but what the hell."

"You know goddam well they won't sell whiskey by the bottle at the bar."

"I do," said Berg simply. "Only four pounds."

McDevin turned on his heel and walked away, feeling slightly ill from his conversation with Sergeant Berg. The sergeant, on the other hand, enjoyed it immensely, and nonchalantly pocketing his ill-gotten gains, he dragged a handkerchief from his side pocket, belched luxuriously, and lazily mopped the grease from his huge fatty jowls. His bluff worked everytime.

When McDevin arrived back in the dining room, he shrugged away the distaste wrought by Sergeant Berg and assumed an air of flippancy, becoming noticeably gayer. With exaggerated carelessness he moved near Linda and laid his hand across her shoulder, dangerously close to her bosom. "Dinner is served in my private dining room in the rear, won't you join me in drinks and steaks—and Crolley, you owe me five pounds."

"Five pounds your metatarsal. I had this thing scientifically calculated early in the evening. How come the twenty rocks?"

"Overhead, chum, overhead."

McDevin took Linda by the hand and led the way past the gloating Sergeant Berg who marched the detail to the storeroom with the potato sacks. The sergeant's rates were usurious, but he was proud of his clandestine cuisine and had gone all out for his latest sucker. The table was laid with the best GI medical department crockery. There were candles, also provided by the government. Potato sacks had been moved judiciously close to the table, and cases of powdered milk, piled one on top of the other, served as a makeshift bar. Mike and Dick helped their girls be seated and Sergeant Berg belched softly and hiccoughed. "Your chow'll be here in a minute."

Dick, who was usually overloquacious, had been strangely silent since he had spied Doris in the crowd, and now for the first time he resumed his role of the clown with, "And now that we are away from the rabble and the peasants, let us gorge ourselves with food and drink! Let us worship at the Tabernacle of Bacchus! And let us genuflect before the Goddess of Love."

"Oh, dry up, you talk too much," said Mike. "I should waste my time listening to you gab when I can make love to a beautiful woman."

"Rather self-assured, aren't you, Lieutenant? Neither the candles nor the potato sacks arouse a bit of passion in my breast. Although I should very much like to eat, I shouldn't hesitate a moment to leave these beautiful steaks, which apparently cost you ten pounds, to go back to the dining room with a relative guarantee of safety for the remainder of the evening and repast on eggs and spam."

"Oh, Linda, quit being so artificial," exclaimed Doris. "You know bloody well that you'd do anything for steaks these days."

Sergeant Berg's cuisine was directly counter to his grammar

31

and the food he had prepared would have been highly acceptable anywhere. The meal passed with the usual dinner-table patter and was climaxed by a cigarette and a double scotch-and-soda all around.

Draining her second highball, Linda remarked, "These potato sacks are most nerve-wracking. Let's go back and dance."

"If you wish," acquiesced Mike, and they left Crolley and Doris amidst barren plates, a half-emptied bottle of Scotch and a storeroom half-filled with potato sacks.

Once back at the party, they took advantage of the bouncing and jive of the GI band which was on its fifth go-around of *Black Magic.*

"I'm awfully sorry, Linda, about what happened earlier. I hope you don't think too badly of me."

Linda murmured something indistinguishable in his ear and McDevin held her tightly.

"Shall we go for a walk? I promise to guide you away from the annex," whispered McDevin, running his hand deliciously up and down Linda's back.

She slowly stroked the nape of his neck and kissed him lightly below his ear.

McDevin danced toward the door and drew Linda into the arms of the deep, purple night. They walked down the path from the officers' club and across the miniature square by the commanding officer's concrete blockhouse, stopping now and then to embrace.

"I like your shoes," remarked McDevin, for want of something better.

"That's an odd thing to say at a time like this. They are very ordinary shoes." But unable to resist the needle of ego, she stopped and lifted a trim foot forward from the ground to demonstrate her very attractive legs and ankles.

"You haven't told me where you live."

"So I haven't. My home is Cambridge, just thirty kilometers away. My address is Causewayside. I would so much like to have you visit me. I share a flat with my mother, but she goes to bed early and I think you'd rather enjoy spending the night with me." And then, after a deliberate hesitation, she added, "You can sleep in my brother's room. He's away in Africa with the Eighth. He's a lieutenant of ordnance."

"I've got to fly a few missions first, but as soon as I can get a pass I'll let you know, and we can have a party."

By now they were just outside the door of the annex, and since Linda offered no resistance, McDevin led her inside. It was completely dark except for the small splashes of the twilight of the English summer evening. It was nearing eleven.

"You *do* like me a little bit, don't you, Mike?" cooed Linda, as she pressed her body close to his.

McDevin breathed heavily. "Of course, I do, darling," and his lips sought hers. His hands searched for her breasts, but she pulled away. She arranged her long, slim body gracefully on a nearby GI cot and stretched comfortably. She moaned softly, like the sea, easily buffing the sands of a Pacific island beach. McDevin sat down. His breath came short and his heart pounded steadily faster. Blood was violent in his veins and moist hands caressed her body. A half-opened mouth mashed wet lips.

"My God, it must be eleven! The trucks leave at eleven. You'd better take me back to the club!" And Linda slipped from his grasp.

"But hell . . . I thought we were . . . Well, goddamn it, you're not going to quit now?" McDevin's passion turned to anger.

"But Mike, I can't miss my transport. I'd never get back to Cambridge tonight, and I've got to be at my job in the morning."

"Ah, pipe down!" came a voice from across the room. "Take your argument outside."

"You have my address. I'd be delighted to see you again, but really I must be going." Linda moved close and her tongue brushed McDevin's lips. She was gone.

Mike didn't bother to follow. He thrust restless hands deep into his pockets and started for Hut Thirteen. He undressed without ceremony, not even bothering to perform ablutions. As he was crawling into the sack the voice of Canyon floated mockingly from the adjoining bed, "Brother can you spare ten pounds?"

*　　*　　*

It was seven o'clock the next morning when Bill Canyon, having left the previous night's party early, sprang from bed and prepared to make life miserable for his two companions. After a quick survey he discovered he would have to be content with

33

tantalizing just one, since Crolley had seen fit to remain away all night. His bed was unslept in and his bags and toilet articles remained in complete disarray, as was his habit. Bill plugged in his DC wireless and turned it on full blast to Armed Forces Radio where a GI disc jockey was spinning *Black Magic*. He dressed quickly, then picked up an empty coal bucket and ash shovel and with exaggerated deliberance lifted it even with his shoulders and let it drop to the floor, smashing and clattering at the head of McDevin's bed.

"Rise and shine, Clementine. It's a beautiful day in Jolly Old England. The fog is everywhere." He jerked the covers from McDevin and threw them upon Crolley's bed, then picked up the coal bucket and beat it rhythmically, keeping time with the dying strains of *Black Magic*. When that ended, he began an ill-conceived tattoo, resembling a bolero.

"You dirty bastard! You're not à goddamn bit clever. Give me back my covers. I'm freezing." McDevin was furious.

"You didn't mind laying bare-assed last night, so why should it bother you now?" taunted Canyon.

"It is my displeasure to report to you, Lieutenant Canyon, that last night was a complete and dismal failure. All I got was teased. I should've let you have the old whore when you wanted her so bad. It would have served you right."

"Now, now, Mike, my boy, let's not be bitter. 'Tis better to have fought and lost, than not to have fought at all."

"Don't you mean loved instead of fought? You're the dumbest man I know; besides I hate your guts. Now what the hell good did it do you to wake me up at this ungodly hour? And give me back my covers before I get up and scratch your eyes out."

"But Clementine, you look so ravishing, lying there in that union suit. It's a shame to cover it up."

"Go to hell."

Canyon grabbed hold of McDevin's feet and began dragging him out of bed.

"What the hell do you think you're doing, you big ape?" screamed McDevin.

"Just checkin', just checkin'," Bill laughed, and McDevin landed with a thud on the floor. He grabbed a coal shovel and began to chase Canyon out of the hut when a bleary-eyed Crolley listlessly dragged himself through the door.

"Well, if it ain't lover boy," said Canyon. "The poor little darling's been out all night. Naughty, naughty."

Crolley threw himself down on his bunk, heaved a long sigh, and said in a well-modulated tone, "William, you have long ago ceased to mean anything in my life. So far as I'm concerned, you could suddenly turn into a cabbage to be plucked and devoured by a roving scavenger, never again to blemish the surface of this world of ours. Begone, knave. Out of my sight. If I want you I'll ring."

"Just keep talking, Shakespeare," laughed Canyon. "I thought we might get a little ditty on the radio for your enjoyment this morning, Rover Boy. Some hit tune like *Onward Christian Soldiers* or *The Old Rugged Cross* or maybe even *Black Magic*."

"Goddamn it, Bill, turn that thing off," begged McDevin. "Can't you see I'm a sick man? I might even die."

"I hope you do," said Crolley, as he stretched out. "The quicker the world is rid of you rabble, the better off we Aryans will be."

"What have you got to be so high and mighty about?" protested McDevin. "All I saw you do last night was follow that little brown-eyed prostitute around with a sick-calf look on your face."

"How crude, and for your information that 'little brown-eyed prostitute' is not a prostitute at all, but rather a sporting lady, shall we say. The Bohemian type. While you have been down here, living in sin with the likes of Canyon all night, I have been up at the annex living in sin with a body beautiful. Ah, *l'amour, l'amour*."

"Ain't it disgustin'?" said Canyon in mocked abhorrence.

McDevin lit a cigarette, pulled out what remained of Canyon's bottle, poured a drink all the way around, and said, "Well, would you condescend to tell us the story surrounding this sex orgy, or do we have to beat it out of you?"

"I detest violence," said Crolley dramatically. "I'll be glad to tell you each beautiful part of the greatest love scene of all time. If you recall my favorite adage, one which I have ofttimes repeated to your yokel ears, 'Them which has, gits.' I had it and I got it. Those sacks of potatoes were damned hard. So for a pittance, Sergeant Berg told me about those bunks in the annex. I took Old Round Heels down there, and there we were for the

35

rest of the night. Can you imagine it boys? She actually seduced me! Me! The very bulwark of decent living."

"Laugh, laugh," smirked McDevin. "Now tell us what really happened."

"Well, if you must know, she left me for some bombardier from the 837th Squadron and I got stupid drunk. On the way home I must have passed out, because when I woke up this morning I was lying on the floor inside the door of the annex. I don't mind missing my fun so much, but what gripes the hell out of me is that I was only ten feet from a bed, and some son of a bitch laid me on the floor. All of which leads me to believe that the *esprit de corps* of this outfit stinks. There ought to be a regulation that when officers pass out they should be tucked in a comfortable bed some place and not left inside doorways on floors." Crolley yawned and added, "Speak to the chaplain on that for me, will you, Canyon? That would be a good job for a baboon like you. And now, if you will excuse me, I shall rest my tired bones between these satin sheets, and so far as I'm concerned you can both go to hell."

McDevin looked at Canyon. He smiled and began, "Salvation Army, Salvation Army, throw a nickel on the drum, save another drunken bum," all the while beating the coal bucket with a strong-measured tempo. Just then Captain Skilling, the squadron operations officer, opened the door.

"I hate to bust up this nice little party, boys, but in case you don't know it, we got a training schedule to meet and the quicker you get it done, the quicker you start on your missions."

"I'm in no hurry," said Crolley.

"No, I don't imagine you are," retorted Skilling. "But nobody is. The sooner you get started, the sooner you can go home. Canyon, I'm sending you on your first mission tomorrow. You'll ride co-pilot to Lieutenant Griggs. That is, if we're not stood down. The next time you're on your own. I'm sorry we haven't been able to give you guys any simulated-combat training flights, but we've lost so damn many airplanes lately that we just couldn't do it."

"Isn't that gay?" smirked Crolley.

"I know how you feel, but you're no better than anybody else. I'll dig up a co-pilot and fly you guys on a wing for a couple of missions; then I'm going to give you an element lead. If you work out I'll make a lead crew out of you. According to your records you're pretty hot."

"I thought Griggs was lead crew," stated Canyon. "And if he is, I'll have to ride in the tail. Doesn't the air leader ride in the right seat?"

"Usually, but Griggs is almost finished with his tour and we're going to fly him deputy tomorrow. We'll be low squadron and he's perfectly capable of taking over in case the leader gets knocked out."

"I don't mind doing it, Captain, but I've never flown a combat mission before and I don't know if I can take over an airplane flying lead position. Griggs would have all he could do as command pilot."

"I know, but we'll just have to take that chance. I got all I can do to get a full squadron in the air, and I hate to break up another crew to get someone to ride that right seat. McDevin, I want you to spend the afternoon on that bomb trainer with Lieutenant Sneith. Crolley, you'd better go across to the GEE trainer and spend a couple of hours. By the way, which one of you is which?"

"I'm McDevin," said Mike. "Pardon the long underwear. Over there on the bed is America's greatest threat to English womanhood, Lieutenant Crolley."

"There's a possibility that I might fly you this afternoon. We have a 'war weary' down on the line that's seen better days and the boys are putting her in commission to fly local stuff. We're going to have to slow-time the engines, so I'll give you a couple of practice bombs and you can go up to the wash and drop them. You'd better start your ground training early today. I'll let you know later if you're going to fly. I want you to check over your flying equipment, too, and make damn sure you have everything. If you don't know now that we're playing for keeps over here, you'll soon learn when a bunch of fighters jump you or you fly through flak. The Krauts got the jump on us in '39 so they have a whole lot more experience than we have. Most of our personnel are green compared with them and the only thing we have more of than they is equipment. You're not playing mumbley-peg. You'd better start thinking about it now. Canyon, check in with me about one o'clock down at operations. Very glad to have met you boys. See you later."

"Hell, I'd practically forgotten about combat," griped Crolley. "All I had to worry about was my hangover."

"I'm sure glad I don't drink," said McDevin.

Captain Skilling's speech had sobered up the boys considerably, and they prepared for the day's training with a slight feeling of anticipation of what was to come in the skies over continental Europe. None of the three had ever admitted to the others that they felt any fear or concern over what might happen. Any reference to their being killed or shot down was made in a joking manner and ostensibly they were as courageous as the next guy. But each of them in his own mind worried to a certain degree, and, like other normal human beings, they were frightened. Canyon, though he sometimes talked a fast game, was actually devoted to his wife and small son and deeply concerned over the future. Crolley had a girl in Ohio whom he intended to marry. McDevin had an almost exaggerated sense of responsibility towards his wife and daughter, and was harassed considerably over the thought of what effect his death might have. All three kept their feelings completely to themselves and never let their worries interfere with their flying, or doing what was required, regardless of the risk.

Psychologically and physically, they were the ideal type for combat aviation. They were all extremely proficient in their respective crew positions, and they worked together magnificently. Their record as a crew left little to be desired, and despite their tendency towards flippancy and their "go to hell" attitude, they were always welcome assets to any operational organization to which they were assigned. In the air, their discipline was impeccable, but on the ground, they allowed themselves to be regimented only enough to keep out of trouble. All three had the abilities necessary for making superior officers, but in this time of strife and danger they recognized their commissions only as a reward for their flying ability and potentials, and tended to be contemptuous, even though they knew they were wrong, of the officers who made up the ground complements of the Air Corps.

Their training was broken up in the middle of the morning, when the operations officer called them down to the line. A replacement airplane, which had arrived a few days before, had been put through a stepped-up, assembly-line-type modification and was ready to be assigned to a crew.

Captain Skilling said: "I have an aircraft for you boys. It's a B-17 G, with a chin turret, number 191. It's parked over on the heartstand near the armament shop. I want you boys to go out and look at it and get familiar with it. You're scheduled for take-off at one o'clock. I'm going to send Hal Barton as instructor-pilot, and you can fly up to the wash. I haven't got the people to brief you, but Hal knows what to do and where to go. I got hold of your engineer this morning and he took the rest of your enlisted personnel to be briefed on our gunnery methods. I don't have to tell you that Jerry sends a few of his fighters over here everyday to pick off the boys who are alone on training missions. I want you to have your crew on the alert at all times. You won't have to test-fire your guns, because I don't like to have a green crew firing any rounds until they get away from the island. You can't tell what you'll hit, but make damn sure they're all loaded and ready to go."

"Where'll I pick up my charts?" asked Crolley.

"Well, since you haven't navigated over here, and since Mc-Devin has never been to our practice area, I'm sending Willy Birtland along with you to ride in the nose. He's a bombardier, but he's done a lot of navigation here, too. So he can help you both. He'll have the charts with him. And McDevin, don't forget to bring your bombing tables and your bombardier kit. For Christ's sake, remember to pick up your metric winds and all the other data you need so you can set up that bombsight. I know you guys know your business, and I don't mean to treat you like a bunch of kids, but so many crews, when they get over here, get kinda confused and they lose their heads even on training missions. I've been talking to the Old Man and looking over our personnel and equipment situation—it looks like we're going to have to fly you guys right away. I want you to be ready tomorrow. Canyon, I'm not going to fly you as co-pilot on somebody's crew. I'm going to make you co-pilot on your own for your first mission, and I'm going to let Barton fly the left seat. Don't get the idea that you're a hot rock because I'm doing this, but from the looks of things I haven't any choice. Griggs is going to fly lead tomorrow and I'm going to put you on his left wing."

"That's a hell of a big order, isn't it, Skilling?" asked McDevin.

"This is a hell of a big war, son," answered Skilling. "Now

you guys jump in that weapons carrier and go on out to the airplane. By the way, everybody names their airplanes here and you can decorate it as you like, but don't put any naked women on it—the Old Man doesn't like it. I don't want to scare you, but don't go to many pains on it because, judging from our past record, it won't last long."

"Oh, jazzy!" said Crolley.

When they arrived at 191 they found a brand-new airplane, completely equipped for combat. The enlisted personnel were already there and each had carefully surveyed his position. McDevin and Crolley crawled into the nose and checked their bombing and navigational equipment, while Canyon went to the flight deck and ran the controls through. After a complete technical perusal of the airplane which found everything in order, the crew had a powwow going over plans for the afternoon's mission.

"What are we going to name dis pig?" asked Terrian, the ball gunner. "How about the Loose Goose?"

"I'm in favor of the Reluctant Virgin," said Dave Rivers, the tail gunner.

"Now wait a minute, fellows," said McDevin, "I'm the last one to discount sex, but this is a pretty serious business. If we're going to name this crate, let's add a little dignity to it. I don't mean we have to name it after a President, or a city, or the Constitution, or anything like that, but let's pick a name that isn't suggestive."

"How about Shoo-Shoo Baby?" suggested Crowley. "It's not too clever, but at least we can write home about it."

"That sounds good to me," said Canyon. "Anybody object to that?"

Nobody did and the airplane was named.

That afternoon Canyon and his crew flew their first and only training flight before a combat mission. It was uneventful, and with the help of the expert guidance of Hal Barton and Willy Birtland, the mission was efficiently completed. Crolley, an expert in his field, demanded little from his instructor, nor did McDevin ask much. Canyon absorbed the new United Kingdom operating procedures as to locations of splasher beacons and forming patterns. The airplane performed to the satisfaction of all crew members and each felt a little safer, knowing that their airplane was a good one and if properly handled would do its part in getting them over the target and back again. That night there was a small red plaque in the window of the orderly room. That meant a Red Alert. The 487th Bomb Group was scheduled for a combat mission the next day. Canyon and his crew were on the availability list.

CHAPTER

4

Corporal Benson made his way in the dark among the huts of the 838th Squadron Area. He was on wake-up detail—not a very pleasant duty. He had a roster of the crews that were scheduled to fly the daily combat mission, and he went methodically to the appropriate huts and aroused the fliers. It was a particularly onerous task, since the hour was early and even under normal circumstances anyone would be reluctant to get up. But when each knew there was a possibility that he would go to his death that day, nearly everyone was in a vile mood. Corporal Benson walked into Hut Number Thirteen and went directly to McDevin's bed. He shook the bombardier and asked, "Are you Lieutenant McDevin?" McDevin had been awake since the trucks began running, carrying the bomb loads to the airplanes.

"Yeah, I'm McDevin."

"Target study at 0200 hours, sir. Special briefing at 0245 in the Group Operations building and a general briefing in the briefing block at 0330. Take-off time at 0500."

"What time is it now?"

"It's 0105, sir. Transportation will leave here for the officers' mess at 0125."

"What's the bomb load," queried McDevin.

"Six one-thousand pounders, sir," answered Benson.

"Did they top off the gas tanks?"

"No, sir," replied Benson. "It's a normal load. Which is Lieutenant Crolley's bed, sir? He has to go, too."

"It's the one right across from me, but I'll wake him up myself. He's a bastard early in the morning."

"Thank you, Lieutenant. I'll come back and wake Lieutenant Canyon at 0200." And Benson left the hut.

McDevin went over to Crolley's bunk and shook him gently. "Wake up, knucklehead. It's time to get your ass shot off."

"I'm happy with my ass like it is," answered Crolley. "Go away and never come back."

"Come on, Dick, and get out of bed. We've got to be at target

42

study at two o'clock. It's almost ten past one already and the trucks leave for the mess at one-thirty."

"I don't see why in the hell I couldn't have been a general or something, or maybe a 4-F; then I wouldn't have to get up in the middle of the night. Gawdamighty, it's cold this early in the morning. I don't think Jerry's going to get a chance to shoot my ass off today 'cause it's going to freeze off before I get dressed."

McDevin and Crolley put on their summer flying suits which they wore under their heavier winter ones, since the temperatures at the high altitude at which they flew sometimes reached fifty degrees below zero. Each grabbed a towel, soap, and a toothbrush and went out to the ablution which was nothing more than a barrel of cold water, some metal washpans, and a drain. Already, some of the others were there. They finished just in time to catch the first truck to the officers' mess hall which was part of the Officers' Club and hurried in to get near the head of the line, since transports were arriving from all squadrons except the 836th which had been "stood down" for training that day. McDevin and Crolley queued behind Willy Birtland.

"This is *it* for you guys today, huh?" said Willy.

"Yeah, how many you got in?" inquired McDevin.

"Fourteen."

"I wonder where we're going today?" asked McDevin.

"Probably to some God-forsaken part of Czechoslovakia," lamented Crolley.

"Uh-huh," said Willy. "We got a full bomb load and a light gas load. That means we're going some place close by. When you got to worry is when you get a light bomb load and a heavy gas load. That means a DP show."

"What the hell's a DP?" asked McDevin.

"Deep penetration," said Birtland, without offering further explanation.

When they got to the steam tables, the KP's gave them powdered eggs and spam with a mug of coffee.

"They're determined to get rid of us, one way or another, aren't they?" griped Crolley. "Either they starve us to death and make us liable to malnutrition from crappy food that you can't eat, or they send you over for the Krauts to slaughter. I should'a stood in Springfield."

"You never had it so good," said Birtland. "By the way, don't

43

forget to take those little boxes at the end of the line. They're filled with concentrated candy that tastes like horse manure, but they sure come in handy on the way home from target."

"Now I'll know how horse manure tastes," said McDevin. "I've always wondered."

"Yeah, you've always had a taste for the stuff," snickered Crolley, then laughed heartily at his own joke.

"I'll bet you guys won't think things are so damn funny the next time they schedule you for a mission. You don't see anybody else in the line laughing, do you?" said Birtland.

"I'm just laughing to keep up McDevin's morale," stated Crolley. "He's scared to death."

"Hell, yes, I'm scared," said McDevin. "And so are you, but you won't admit it, you silly bastard. But you might just as well tell me now, 'cause I'll find out from your laundry woman, anyhow."

They ate their meal in relative silence and hurried outside to catch the shuttle bus down to the target room. When they went inside, the group bombardier, Major Bessetti, checked both their names off his list. They were among the first to arrive. He handed them a target folder and told them to look it over while they were waiting for the rest of the bombardiers and navigators. Their target was an airfield at Paris.

"Is this trip really necessary?" cracked Crolley. But no one laughed except McDevin. Soon the room was filled and Major Bessetti began to describe the target and gave them the necessary data to insure a successful mission.

At two forty-five on the dot McDevin and Crolley sat down at special briefing which was reserved for lead and deputy-lead crews. But today, since they expected heavy losses, some of the wing crews of the forward elements were also included. The colonel himself presided at the special briefing. They were given special instructions as to what to do to accomplish the mission. At three o'clock they went to the main briefing block, where they gathered with the rest of the crews, officers in one room and enlisted men in another. McDevin and Crolley sat down by Canyon near the front. An air of presentiment hovered over the room.

"Where are we going today?" asked Canyon.

"Wouldn't you like to know," said Crolley.

"This is no time to be silly," said Bill, with some display of anger.

"Is the big strong man scared?" asked McDevin, as if he were speaking to a very small boy.

"You're goddamn right, I'm scared," said Canyon. "Now stop your damn horseplay or I'll take you outside and knock your heads together."

"You and what army?" snapped Crolley.

"Now, now, children, don't fight," said McDevin. "Bill, if you were real brainy like Crolley and me you could have been a bombardier or navigator and get up at one o'clock like we did for target study and special briefing, but since you're nothing but a dumb pilot you'll just have to wait with the rest of the peasants to find out."

"Nuts," protested Canyon.

"The Old Man told us at special briefing not to tell anybody when we got down here," said McDevin, "because it's a deep, dark secret where we're going. Even General Doolittle doesn't know. But since you're a special friend of ours, we'll tell you. We're going to gay Paree."

"Yeah," said Crolley. "Mike and I thought we'd take in the *Folies Bergere* while we're there. Even at this time of day I could go for a naked woman."

"You could go for a naked woman any time, you oversexed goon," said Canyon disgustedly.

Just then somebody called attention, and the Group commander walked down the aisle and began the briefing.

"Take your seats, gentlemen," said the colonel, and he nodded to a major who pulled a curtain away from the wall, displaying a huge map of Europe with long pieces of colored string denoting courses to the target. There were patches outlined in red all over the map which showed flak areas, and there were pins of various colors indicating fighter concentrations and various enemy installations. "We're going to Paris today," continued the colonel, "to knock out the airfield there. Jerry is using it as a base for fighters and JU-88's. They're giving our troops hell at Cherbourg. Now do your job well—we don't want to have to go back again. We have a few new crews with us today and I want you to listen to the briefing very carefully because we're going to have trouble enough as it is without you guys messing up the detail." He stepped down from the platform and pointed to an officer who got up and presented the target intelligence.

"Gentlemen, your target today is the airfield at Paris, France . . ."

Thirty minutes later, McDevin, Crolley and Canyon left the briefing room.

"How about a cigarette, Mike?" asked Crolley.

"No, thanks, just had an orange."

"Where's the airplane, Bill?" asked Crolley.

"Goddamn it, why didn't you listen? They told us where it was parked," said Canyon irritably.

"What's the matter, Bill, you scared?" asked Crolley.

"Hell, yes, I'm scared."

"I am, too," said Crolley. "And so's everybody else."

The three walked silently to the waiting trucks which would carry them to the drying room and personal equipment storehouse. "Something tells me I should have stayed in Springfield," remarked Crolley with pseudo-gaiety.

"I wonder what my poor old whiskey-drinking wife is doing this morning?" said McDevin.

"Probably out with some strange man," answered Crolley.

"Hell, it's almost noon there now," answered McDevin. "She doesn't start tom cattin' until after sundown."

"You guys are sure sharp this morning. Just like a ball of clay. Why don't you quit trying to impress everybody with your bravery?" said Canyon with sarcasm.

"My dear Lieutenant Canyon," began Crolley, "we of higher intellect tend to look upon things more rationally than those such as you. We are not prone to be frightened by a few paltry German fighter attacks or enemy anti-aircraft fire; rather, we are inclined to take a more intelligent view and are eager to pit our wits against those of the so-called super-race. Furthermore, jughead, if you think I'm going to start singing the blues at a time like this, you're wrong. I'm just trying to fool myself and I'm very happy with my efforts. I am basically a coward, you broadshouldered chimpanzee, and I'm scared spitless. Now you just mind your guts and I'll mind mine."

The GI truck ground to a noisy stop in front of the brown, dirty building in which the aviators' flying togs were stored. It consisted of one large room filled with lockers in which each individual stored his personal flying suit and allied accouterment. In the rear of the building was another good-sized room called the drying room. Here electrical flying suits were stored between missions to prevent damage by the British Isle's perennial dampness. But more important than electrical flying suits to many of the men was a small, makeshift cubbyhole in the corner of that room. In it was Father Guilfoyle, the Catholic chaplain. He gave communion to the Catholics and passed his blessing to the Protestants and Jews on every mission. Very few passed up his booth. He never missed being there for he knew that many depended upon Him more than upon their aircraft.

McDevin, Crolley, and Canyon had lockers adjacent to one another. They went first to pick up their electrical flying suits, then to Father Guilfoyle, though none were Catholics, and finally to the locker room where they dressed in preparation for their mission. McDevin and Canyon immediately began to dress and carefully check the electrical connections among the upper and lower halves of their flying suits and their electrically heated flying boots. They meticulously adjusted their .45 pistols in shoulder holsters. Concentrated candy packed in plastic cases was fitted into huge pockets on the shins of their flying trousers. They gathered helmets, ear phones, oxygen masks, and all the other paraphernalia peculiar to the combat flyer, including escape kits which contained French francs, rubberized-silk charts, fish hooks and compasses. Crolley sat down on the floor, leaned leisurely against his locker and nonchalantly drew on a cigarette.

"You'd better start dressing, Dick. You can't do everything at once and we've got to check the ship when we get out there," said Canyon.

"I should waste my time yet. Suppose we get the red flare and don't fly a mission, then all this will have been for nothing. No, I'll wait till we get off the ground."

"It's your funeral," said Canyon with resignation.

"Thank you for your concern, Father," replied Crolley. "I got everything in this nice bag and I'll heave it on the truck and carry it out to the airplane. Then I'll check that beauty over and while you're up there working your behind off, starting the engines and taxiing in position for take-off, I shall exercise my prerogative as a navigator, a genius in my own right, a man of superior intellect, and take my time preparing for the bloody battle."

"Crolley, sometimes you make me sick," said Canyon vehemently.

"Well, don't throw up on me, sonny, there's lots of room outside," answered Crolley with a laugh. "You take things too damn seriously, Bill. This is just the first one. We got a long ways to go yet. What's the sense of wearing yourself out?"

"All right, wise guy, I'll see you out at the airplane," said Canyon and walked away.

"What the hell's the trouble with him?" asked Crolley.

"You shouldn't needle him, Dick," admonished McDevin. "Bill always wants to do things right. This is a serious business with him just like any other job he's ever had. He thinks he is personally responsible for all the rest of us on the crew. And he is. So you gotta kinda cooperate with him and make him think you're helping him out. You know damn well you wouldn't fly with any other pilot. I don't care how much you raise hell myself, but I think I understand you a little better than he does, so what do you say we save our horseplay till a little later?"

"You should have been a Baptist, Mike," said Crolley, as he mashed out his cigarette and picked up his huge bag.

"Why do you say that?" asked McDevin.

"Because you don't stop sinning; you just keep people from enjoying it. Okay, bright eyes, I'll do what you say, but I'm not going to turn into a sad Sammy just for Canyon. Tell you what I'll do. I'll meet you halfway. Instead of all the horseplay, I'll start acting like a jackass like you."

"Okay, jackass, let's get the hell out to the airplane."

It was a good ten minutes going around the perimeter of the airfield before they arrived at 191. Canyon was already there, busily checking all enlisted crew positions, running through the controls, and making a superficial, but thorough, survey of the condition of the aircraft's four engines and landing gear. McDevin and Crolley crawled into the nose, McDevin setting up the bombsight and Crolley languidly going over his navigational equipment.

"Like to have me explain that complicated stuff to you, Crolley?" asked McDevin tauntingly.

"Drop dead," replied Crolley.

McDevin set the pertinent, complex data into his intricate

bombsight and then went back to the bomb bay to arm the bombracks. As bombardier he was also oxygen officer and was in charge of the ship's gunnery. He checked all the crew members to see that their guns were properly installed and then proceeded to the front of the airplane where he inserted his two fifty-caliber machine guns into the aircraft's chin turret. Canyon was checking the turbo-supercharger of number two engine.

"Too bad we're not going to fly today, Bill," commented Mike, as he inserted the buffer plate on his second gun.

"I thought we were," said Canyon, carefully scrutinizing number two engine.

"Well, according to my latest head count," continued McDevin, "we're minus one pilot. I didn't even see him in briefing."

"He was in the drying room while you were in chinning with Holy Joe. We still have five minutes before engine time."

Just then two green flares emanated from the field's tower, indicating that the mission would be flown as briefed. Concurrently a jeep came to a screaming halt in front of the aircraft and out jumped Hal Barton. He was a red-faced, happy-go-lucky chap from Los Angeles with the reputation for being the most technically perfect pilot in the entire group. He was also considered to be the most scatter-brained. He wore a perpetual smile on his face and a combat mission to him was nothing more than a Sunday afternoon drive in the park. He got excited when he was jumped by enemy fighters or his aircraft was hit by flak, but he also got excited when he won at bingo or when a fire whistle blew.

"Hey, Bill, hey! Have you got the engines checked? Is everything ready to go? Is all the crew here? How about the bombs? Let's go, let's go!" The flow of words from Hal Barton, half in desperation, half in despair, carried just a touch of his feeling that he should say something as a pilot to his crew. An oil-stained flying jacket was unbuttoned and dog tags fluttered around his head as he ran toward the airplane. Both Bill and McDevin tried to answer his array of questions, but Hal had already pulled himself through the forward door of the B-17's fuselage and was well on his way to the flight deck.

The crew was in position, ready to take off on mission number one. Each was anticipatory of the danger that was to come.

McDevin and Crolley tried to fend off any fright they might develop by their usual wit and absurdities. Canyon was silent, with his mind strictly on business. Porky Terrian, the ball-turret gunner, repeated several "Hail Marys," and Dave Rivers, the tail gunner, thought about home, his face shiny with despair. Gordon Goud, the radio operator, checked his equipment over and over, to make sure everything was all right. Ken Jones, the waist gunner, was just plain scared and didn't mind telling people about it. Jack Rhodes, the engineer, scrutinized the instruments repeatedly and double-checked his upper-turret guns. He braced himself between pilot and co-pilot and gritted his teeth in determination.

Hal and Bill expertly lined 191 with the runway. Like most British flying fields, it was short, and the heavy-laden bombers found it difficult to get off the ground before they ran out of traction space. Hal put on the brakes firmly, flaps were down, and the gas mixture was full rich. He thrust the throttles forward and as the engines screamed with full power he suddenly released the brakes and the big B-17 lurched down the runway. At first it stuck tenaciously to the ground, but soon the tail began to rise reluctantly and the machine prepared to pull away from the stubborn terrain. McDevin and Crolley watched the far end of the runway come closer and closer. McDevin, as if trying to help the pilot, pulled silently on an imaginary stick, and just when he thought they were going to crash over the runway's edge into a green English meadow, 191 defeated gravity and lifted itself into the air. Bill reached over with a moist hand and flipped the switch that retracted the landing gear. Now that the aircraft was airborne and had gained momentum, Hal throttled back ever so slightly to ease the strain on the laboring engines. The airplane pointed its nose just above the horizon and pulled itself steadily and relentlessly away from the ground and into the "wild blue yonder."

Crolley navigated toward Splasher Seven at Braintree, the initial point of rendezvous for the group. At ten thousand feet, McDevin, who was in charge of oxygen aboard the aircraft, ordered the crew to put on its oxygen masks and asked for an oxygen check. Both Bill and Hal were experts in maneuvering and quickly slid into place as number three ship in the high squadron. The group flew a zigzag course over the eastern part of England, careful to keep its time schedule to the second. As the bomber stream left the coast, headed toward France, the 487th Group fell into position. They were at fifteen thousand feet and gaining altitude at the rate of two hundred feet per minute. Midway over the English Channel, Crolley called the crew over the interphone: "Navigator to crew, navigator to crew. We'll be over the coast of France in about ten-and-a-half minutes. At that time we'll be greeted by grandiose display of flak. It's Jerry's way of welcoming us to gay and turbulent Europe. Check your flak suits to make sure they are on properly, and those of you who have chest packs, keep them within easy reach."

McDevin squinted through the nose of the ship through tinted goggles. Ahead, he could make out small black puffs that dotted the air like spots before his eyes. They took on a particularly sinister shape, although they appeared to be harmless. To an esthetic soul, they might be quite pleasing to the eye. Hal's strained voice came over the intercom: "Pilot to crew, pilot to crew. Okay, boys, this is it. Now don't get excited. Everything's going to be all right. As long as you can see them, it won't hurt you. It's the ones you can't see that you should be afraid of. Hey, Mike, make an oxygen check, will you?"

McDevin obeyed instantly. "Bombardier to crew, bombardier to crew. Oxygen check," and response from the crew was quick and crisp.

"Tail gunner, Roger."

"Left-waist gunner, Roger."

"Right-waist gunner, Roger."

And so on through the entire crew.

The oxygen check was supposed to be made frequently, since a leak in the oxygen system, or in an individual's mask, or punctured oxygen tanks or lines as a result of enemy action, could cause a crew member to be overcome by that insidious demon anoxia, and slip quietly and unknowingly into the soft, mysterious arms of death. For death was a constant companion of the combat crew and took its toll in many ways.

Valiant 191 entered her first flak field only to be rebuffed forcibly by the intensity and viciousness of the German 88's. Her skin was riddled by the vicious little pellets thrown maliciously helter-skelter by innocent-looking black puffs. The radio operator pushed quantities of metalized paper called "chaff" through a small chute in the side of the aircraft. The chaff was cut in small strips and looked like the imitation icicles with which kids decorated their trees at Christmas time. Its purpose was to jam the electronically controlled aiming devices of the Germans' highly developed antiaircraft guns. The squadron air leader guided his ships in a slightly zigzag course, a form of evasive action which made more difficult the task of the German gunners to bracket in their targets.

Suddenly, when the flak was dense around them, the right wingman of the lead element lurched and swung suddenly upward and then went into a crazy spin and sped toward the ground, out of control. Its right wing had been shattered and blown away. McDevin and Crolley watched for parachutes. There were two, then another, and finally one more, and then the doomed aircraft was but a speck against a crosspatch of the fields below.

"Oh, hell," muttered McDevin.

And then as if to strengthen its determination, the flak became more intense. There was a loud explosion beneath 191. She swayed crazily from the impact. Her fuselage from the wings aft was like a sieve from the evil, red-hot projectiles.

The ball gunner screamed over the intercom, "I'm hit, I'm hit bad. Somebody get me out of here."

"Co-pilot to radio operator, co-pilot to radio operator," came Canyon's even voice. "Roll the ball up manually and get Terrian out of there. See how badly he's hurt and report. All the rest of you keep your positions."

"Radio operator to co-pilot, Roger," croaked Gordon Goud.

"Engineer to pilot, engineer to pilot. Your oil pressure's down on number one."

"Gotcha," came back Hal.

The antiaircraft was subsiding and the 487th Bomb Group tightened its formation. McDevin called for an oxygen check and Crolley found himself on his dead-reckoning chart. The authoritative voice of the squadron air leader sounded over VHF: "The group just ahead was hit by bandits. Let's tighten up the formation. All gunners be on the alert."

"Radio operator to pilot. I got Porky out of the ball, Lieutenant. He just got a slight flesh wound in his shoulder. It bled pretty bad at first, but I poured some sulfa powder in it and wrapped it up. He's going back in the ball in a minute."

"Roger," answered Hal. "All you guys keep your eyes open. Be on the lookout for enemy fighters, probably ME 109's. They have been comin' in at twelve o'clock lately and a few from the tail. You all set with that chin turret, Mike?"

"Roger," answered McDevin. "This is a helluva way to make a living."

"Bandits, twelve o'clock," screamed the engineer, and began blasting away with his upper turret. But the rate of closure was so great between the two aircraft that McDevin didn't even get the fighter in his turret sight. It was an ME 109 coming in head on, all guns blazing. And just when a crash seemed imminent it skillfully evaded 191, turned over gracefully on its back, and then, straight and level once again, started its climb for another attack. McDevin was more fortunate on his next two. They came from twelve o'clock high in echelon. The bombardier was surprisingly cool, and just as they were positioned well in his sight ring he let go a full burst, seriously damaging the lead aircraft. Terrian, who by this time was back in his ball, was having a field day. He didn't bother to call the positions of the oncoming fighters, but simply proceeded to unload round after round with dire effect. He finished off the one that McDevin had wounded and turned his attention to a flight of four which was crossing underneath the formation. He got another kill.

Contrary to past record, the fighter attack was shortlived and the 487th ground forward towards the target, with the worst damage done to 191. Part of the right stabilizer was shot away and the entire fuselage was a mass of holes. Now that the danger was past, McDevin called for an oxygen check. All was well except for the tail gunner whose oxygen supply has been shot out and who had gone on a small emergency bottle. McDevin ordered him to the waist to plug into the main supply.

"Navigator to pilot," said Crolley. "It should be easy going from here to the IP if we follow the brief course and if Jerry hasn't changed his antiaircraft installations."

"Roger," said Hal.

Crolley's statement proved to be true. There was only light flak and no fighters for the remainder of the inward trip until they neared Paris. But the crew was constantly on the alert.

McDevin began to prepare to bomb. Since he was not in the lead ship his only concern was to release the bombs at the proper time depending upon the lead bombardier for the correct course. The IP was a bend in the river Seine, just below the point where the river Epte joins it. McDevin checked his bomb station indicators and his bombsight to make sure that everything was in order.

Light flak began as they turned on the IP and increased in intensity the nearer they got to Paris. McDevin opened the electrically controlled, bomb-bay doors, buried his head in his bombsight, and as soon as the target was visible he went into action. The course of the lead bombardier was good and, with his own manipulations, McDevin kept his rate crosshair on the point of impact. Flak was becoming intense and two more ships in the squadron were hit badly. One of them went down in flames and the other dropped from formation, headed away from the flak field and turned toward home. To the crew of 191, each second seemed like hours and the whole crew experienced a feeling of relief and elation when McDevin said, "Bombs away."

The radio operator switched on the camera which would record the impact, and then peered into the darkness of the bomb bay to ascertain if any bombs remained. He reported to McDevin that all was clear, and the bombardier closed the doors. The group turned abruptly off the target and gained air speed by losing altitude. Once away, they tightened their formation and started the homeward trek. Nine ships remained of the original thirteen in the 838th Squadron.

* * *

Mission number one was over. The crew sat at an interrogation table, answering the questions put to them by a red-faced, bald-headed captain of Intelligence. They reported times, altitudes, probable target damage, and enemy action. The interrogator, as a civilian, had been a lawyer in Philadelphia. He was a jovial chap and well liked by the other officers of the group. But interrogation was getting old to him, since he had been engaged in it for almost a year. His questions were asked in a monotone and he gave the impression that he didn't care a great deal whether they answered or not. Throughout the entire proceedings McDevin and Crolley practiced their usual garrulity, while the others answered the questions that were put to them as briefly as possible and smoked cigarettes.

"How was the flak over the target?" asked the captain.

"Intense and unbearable," piped Crolley with a snicker.

"Oh, get you," said Canyon to Crolley; then continued to the interrogating captain, "It was pretty rough."

"Hell, I know that," said the captain, impatiently. "Can't you be more specific?"

"Goddamn it, Captain," snapped McDevin. "How do you expect us to be specific? This is our first mission. I don't know whether you call the flak we saw intense, light, or indifferent. All I know is the sky was filled with crap. I saw four airplanes go down and we got a million and one holes in our ship. If you're so damn curious, why in the hell didn't you go yourself?"

"I'm too old and fat," grinned the captain. "And besides, I'm bald."

"I'm sorry I blew my stack," said McDevin, sheepishly, "but I got the hell scared out of me today. Better let Hal tell you about it. He's an old hand at this game."

"What about it, Hal?" asked the captain. "I've interrogated you three or four times before and you've never told me a damn thing. What can you do this time?"

Hall sucked deeply on his cigarette and laughed. "Well, counselor, I'd say it was intense, mostly 88's and a few 105's. Jerry was pretty accurate today, but he always is around Paris. If you want to fill in the other blanks, I can tell you we were at 24,000 feet and we were indicating about 155 over the target. As far as I can figure out, the winds were as briefed, about thirty-five knots from two-hundred degrees. Isn't that right, Crolley?"

Crolley nodded acquiescence.

The interrogator quickly and efficiently recorded the information and asked, "Any battle damage?"

Canyon spoke up. "Number one engine is done for. She leaked oil from the time we hit France on. Our right stabilizer is almost off and the whole airplane is pretty well filled with holes. She won't fly again without a lot of work and maybe not then. Number three engine isn't much good either, and number four prop is all nicked to hell. We had to pull full power to keep up from the time we left the target until we hit the channel, then we dropped from formation and came in on the deck."

"Who's the bombardier?" asked the interrogator.

"I'm the genius," said McDevin. "What do you want to know? Just ask me."

"Oh, it's you, hotbead. Okay, smarty pants. Tell me about the bomb run."

"Well, in the first place, it was too goddamn long. The IP was too far away and we were going almost into the wind. It took us twelve minutes from the time I opened the bomb-bay doors till we got to the target. Course was good and my rate was right on the button because my bombs went away the same time as the lead bombardier's did."

"Didn't anyone ever tell you you were just supposed to toggle the bombs and leave those damn knobs alone, except when you have to take over the lead?" asked the interrogator with some irritation.

"Listen, Perry Mason, I don't mean to be disrespectful toward your age or your rank, but I wasn't commissioned to sit and flip a switch. I'll stack my bombing against any other bombardier's in the group. Those bastards sent me through bombardier's school against my will and now that they've had their fun, I'll be damned if I'll be cheated out of using what I know."

"Well, I'm not going to argue with you here, that's up to your squadron commander. Do you think you hit the target?"

"Yeah, I think we got some pretty good strikes, but I got a .couple suggestions to make to you. First of all, shorten the bomb run. When you open those bomb-bay doors, it creates a hell of a drag on the airplane and slows you down considerably. And besides, you can't pick up the target, even with the bombsight's extended vision, twelve minutes away. Furthermore, why in the name of Christ did we go against the wind? It took twenty knots away from our ground speed."

"I don't make the rules, sonny," said the interrogating officer, "but your suggestion sounds sensible to me, about the length of the bomb run, I mean. But they had a special reason for going against the wind today. If you had come in from the south on that target, you would have lost a hell of a lot more than four airplanes because of the location of their antiaircraft defenses. They weren't expecting us to hit the airfield. Why? I don't know. You got anything else you want to yap about?"

"Nothing else now, Captain, except for one thing. They tell

me the medics are doling out whiskey to us poor, flak-happy combat boys. I was wondering if you'd just kinda aim me, that is, if you're through with the direct and cross-examination."

"Well, I haven't got any more questions. Anybody got anything to add?" And he looked inquiringly at each member of the crew. "Well, since there are no takers, you'll find the booze in the little room just outside the main briefing room. See you next mission. Maybe tomorrow."

"Drop dead," said Crolley, as he followed in the wake of Mc-Devin, hurrying toward the free whiskey. When they reached the medical bartenders, Dick asked, "Any limit on this stuff?"

"Yes, sir. One to each crew member. Please sign your name here with the others," said the attendant courteously, as he poured an ounce-and-half-shot glass full for each of them. "However," he continued, "if you know someone who doesn't drink and won't take his shot, you can put his name down and drink it for him."

"I know a thousand people," said McDevin. "There's Uncle Bert, cousin Charlie, old man Ingstrom, and the Madam who runs the house down on Clay Street and Second Avenue in my home town. They're all teetotalers. Hell, just give me a fifth." There was a twinkle in his eye.

The attendant started to explain that he meant combat-crew members.

"Yeah, I know. I was just kiddin'," smiled McDevin.

"Well, Mike," said Crolley, as he lifted his glass, "here's to the girl who lives on the hill; she won't, but her sister will."

"Here's to her sister," answered McDevin. He swallowed his drink. "Fill 'em up again, bartender. Crolley, you sign Canyon's name, and I'll sign Hal's."

"You're leading me astray, Mike, but I have no will power. I should like to propose another toast. Here's to Hans, may he die in a fit of passion."

"Who's Hans?" asked McDevin, as he threw down the bourbon.

"Remember when we got hit on the coast of France, near Calais? Well, Hans is the guy who pulled the trigger. Private Hans Finklemeyer."

"Good old Hans," said McDevin. "Now I'll sign Joe Doaks and you sign Richard Roe's name. Fill 'em up, bartender."

"I'm sorry, sir, but there are a number of people in line

behind you. I don't mind your drinking, but I can't pass out too much or I'll run out of liquor. Then there'll be hell to pay."

"Can't you see we're suffering from battle fatigue? I'm a nervous wreck. We're both wrecks. We need a stimulus, for tomorrow we may fly again. Come, come, man, enough of this dilly-dally."

"Well, okay," said the attendant, dubiously, "but this is the last one. Now, if you'll just take these two and step aside so I can serve the rest of the guys, you'll help me out a lot."

"I always strive to be helpful," said McDevin, as he and Crolley moved aside. "Lieutenant Crolley, may I propose a toast? Pardon me while I wax academic. Here's to pure water. 'Pure water is the best of drinks, that man to man can bring; but who am I to have the best of anything? Let princes revel at the pump, let peers with ponds make free; but whiskey, wine, or even beer is good enough for me.' Skoal."

An hour later, McDevin, Crolley, and Canyon were in hut number thirteen in various degrees of undress. Bill, who had been flying formation most of the day, an activity which entails considerable physical exertion, was dead tired and was preparing for bed. McDevin and Crolley, though equally as tired, were preparing to go to the bar.

"One of you simple bastards owes me a drink," said Canyon in indignation. "I had a hell of a time convincing the medics that I should have a shot, even though they knew somebody else had already signed my name. Now which one of you is the culprit?"

"Lieutenant Canyon," began Crolley with pseudo-dignity, "you have alleged that either Lieutenant McDevin or myself fraudulently used your name to obtain a commodity, namely, one shot each of 'Old Toiletseat,' an insidious drink designed by the United States Government to completely burn out your guts. They have carefully calculated that by taking one drink of 'Old Toiletseat' after each mission, the average combat flier, by the time he has finished a tour of combat duty—assuming he lives through it— will die what appears to be a natural death, thus saving the American taxpayers the expense of transporting him home. A sly trick. Your allegation amounts to a false accusation which is a violation of something or other and makes you liable to prosecution and trial by court-martial. Have you proof to back up your charges?"

"Hell, yes, I got proof. I saw my name on that whiskey list," said Canyon. "And quit trying to be funny. Besides, the bartender told me it was a couple of baboons like you."

"My dear Canyon," said McDevin, "that is strictly hearsay and will not stand up in court. You are simply grasping for straws. It is nothing more than an underhanded attempt to extort admission of a dastardly deed from Lieutenant Crolley and myself. If you continue to reiterate these false accusations, Lieutenant Crolley and myself will find it necessary to take punitive action. I suggest that you desist immediately, else you'll wake up some fine morning and find yourself castrated."

"Horse manure," spat Canyon.

"Well!" exploded Crolley in mock anger, "I never!"

"All I got to say," continued Canyon smugly, "is that the both of you suffer from an acute case of constipation of the brain and diarrhea of the mouth."

Crolley and McDevin looked at each other. "He couldn't have thought that up himself," said Crolley.

"You guys can't take it," accused Canyon. "You can sure dish it out, but you can't take it. Now if you two will kindly go to hell, I'm going to bed. And please don't wake me up when you come in tonight. And for your information, and I'm sorry I forgot to tell you before, especially now that you're all dressed and ready to go out, there's a small, red, square board in the orderly-room window, which means we gotta fly tomorrow. Good-night."

McDevin and Crolley were silent and began quietly to undress.

"What time is it, Dick?" asked McDevin.

"Seven o'clock," answered Crolley.

"When was the last time you were in bed this early?" queried McDevin.

"Remember that carnival in Kearney, Nebraska? The one with the big blue eyes and the swivel hips?"

"Yeah."

"Well, one night while we were there she put me to bed, against my will, of course, in her house-trailer. Isn't it funny, Mike? I worried like hell that night how I was going to get back before lights out, and about the chewin' I'd get the next day from the Old Man in case I was late. It all seems so insignificant now, because tomorrow I have to worry about gettin' the hell shot out of me. You know, Mike, the more I think about this guy Einstein, the more right he appears to be. Everything is relative."

"Why so philosophical all of a sudden?" asked McDevin. "That doesn't sound like you."

"I'll tell you why, Mike. I'm scared to death. I don't want to fly tomorrow."

"I don't either, Dick. You're not the only one who's scared, but I'll tell you one thing, I gotta feelin' we're going to get through this mess all right."

"Do you know how to pray, Mike?" asked Crolley.

"Sure, don't you?"

"Yeah. I hope you don't think I'm silly. What do you say we mention a few holy words. I think the Lord's fed up with us, anyway. It wouldn't hurt us a damn bit to say a prayer now and then."

"I don't think you're silly, Dick. I admire you for having the guts to admit that you're afraid and to admit that you want to pray—especially in front of us. Let's say the Lord's Prayer together. You kneel by your bed and I'll kneel by mine and you start it off."

"Wait a minute," came Canyon's voice from across the room. "If you two chaplains are going to talk with the Old Man upstairs I'd kinda like to join you. I've got a few things I'd like to say myself."

The three American youths kneeled down by their beds. The room was dark and the dying embers in the small, pot-bellied stove threw a dim, ghostly light across the floor of Hut Thirteen. The wind outside was quiet, and the trees were bowed in reverence, for these were fliers, and on the morrow death would chase them through the skies. While earthbound mortals were faraway, these lads would soar through clouds and azure blue, and reach out and touch the face of God.

CHAPTER

5

DURING THE NEXT FIVE DAYS MC DEVIN, CROLLEY, AND CANyon flew missions number two and three. It was virtually the same process, with enemy flak and fighters causing considerable damage. One trip was to Metz, near Luxembourg, while the second took them to Cologne in "Happy Valley," the Ruhr, which was the heart of the German industrial area. They used another airplane, since noble 191 had been grounded for major repairs after the foray to Paris.

The trip to "Happy Valley" had been particularly damaging. Intense flak over the target area had taken two crews from the ranks of the 838th Squadron and McDevin's airplane had been turned over to the salvage crew. It was nine o'clock in the morning when McDevin awoke after the tragic journey to Cologne. He yawned sleepily and reached for his cigarettes. His thoughts turned to the previous day's activities, and he shuddered. He relaxed on his hard, straw-filled pillow and dragged on his cigarette. He recalled Osborne's ship in the low squadron receiving a direct hit and blowing up in mid-air—and Osborne on his last mission. And "Stinky" Stanky got it, too. Right over the target. What was the reason for all this killing and destruction? Why? One day you would be laughing and talking with a fellow and the next day you would see him die.

Suddenly he hated Hitler and Germany and the war. Before, it had been a kind of impersonal thing. He knew that there was a Hitler and a Germany and a war—and a Luftwaffe, flak, and prison camps—but they had seemed faraway in another world somehow. Now they were *his* world; they surrounded him and everything he did. Violence and destruction and killing was his way of life—as much as he hated and feared it, he was dedicated to just that. All he was, he knew, was a numbered machine that sat in an airplane and dropped bombs—bombs that were death. And if death turned the tables and claimed him, they would just mark out his number and substitute another.

He mashed out his cigarette, pulled himself laboriously out

of bed, and drew back the blackout curtain a fraction over Canyon's bed.

And then there was Katherine, sweet, unaffected, devoted, unsuspecting Katherine, back home with Mom and Dad. She seemed so far away. He dug out her last letter and began reading by the light from the window. "My darling Mike," he read. "I've been so worried about you lately. I haven't received a letter for nearly two weeks. Everyday I read in the newspapers about all the bombers that the Eighth Air Force is losing. And your Daddy has the radio on all the time he is home and listens to every newscast. It seems your mother has aged ten years since you left. We all pray for you every night. And so does little Susie. Oh, Mike, darling, if anything happens to you, I'll die. I hate to be so morbid, but I just can't help but worry. I should be ashamed of myself for writing this kind of letter, when I should be cheering you up. But my darling, do be careful. I love you so much. . . ."

McDevin reflected over his three years with Katherine. She's the type that would remain faithful to the end, always deeply in love, and would stand by you regardless of who you were, what you were, or what you did. He was luckier than most other fellows, he thought. So many of the officers and enlisted men in his squadron received heartbreaking letters from home, telling them of their wives' infidelity.

Then his face wrinkled with disgust for himself. Linda had interrupted his meditations. He went back over his actions in the annex when he deliberately tried to make her, and he felt ashamed. It was bad enough to do that when you were single, but when you had a nice wife like Katherine, it was unforgivable. He wasn't kidding himself. He knew he was weak and using the old bromide that a combat man is justified in doing that sort of thing. He knew damn well that it was wrong. If Katherine did such a thing he would divorce her in a moment. Why should he think he had any more right to do it than she? But the insatiable desire to savor the essence of sex was deep within him. Even as he cogitated over the wrongness of his actions, thoughts of Linda were exciting the fire of passion that smouldered within his spleen. What manner of man am I? . . .

"I'll bet you're thinking about sex," said Crolley, as he yawned and stretched on his bunk.

"How'd you guess it?" answered McDevin.

"It was easy," replied Crolley. "That's what you think of most of the time. Was there a mission today?"

"Yeah, I heard the trucks rolling about two o'clock and I heard the take-off, too," answered McDevin. "Tomorrow's our stand-down day, by the way. They couldn't have had an airplane for us for today's show. That means we don't fly tomorrow, either."

"They probably had an easy mission today, too," lamented Crolley. "Just our luck. The sooner we get these goddamn missions over, the better I'll like it." And he began dressing.

"Crolley, you stink," said McDevin, wrinkling his nose. "What do you say we go take a shower today?"

"Hell with it," said Crolley. "I don't care if I do stink. I'm not going up and stand under that cold water and freeze my butt. Wait till we go on pass and we get a hotel room some place and then I'll wash this crud off."

"Well, hell, you can at least change clothes," said McDevin. "That might help some."

"What's the use to change clothes till I take a shower?" argued Crolley. "Whoops! Can't hold it any longer. Stand aside, I'm comin' through." He jumped quickly to his feet and ran at full speed to the officers' latrine. When he returned, Canyon was awake, and McDevin was fully dressed, gathering together his dirty laundry. Canyon sat up in bed and said, "Gosh, I'm glad we didn't fly today. I'm beat."

"I'm not so glad," retorted Crolley. "I just saw Skilling out in the can and he says they had a bomb bay full of one-hundred pounders, a light gas load, and they were briefed for low altitude, so that means something on the coast with no opposition. Hell! At this rate we'll never get to go home."

"Aw, quit your bitchin'," said Canyon. "You're no more eager to get done than I am, but you gotta rest sometime. Maybe we can live like human beings for a couple of days. We're stood down tomorrow and maybe if we're lucky the weather will be bad the next day."

"You're just flat lazy," accused McDevin.

"Maybe so," said Canyon, "but that's how I feel about it."

"Say, knucklehead," said Crolley to McDevin, "I've been thinking over your allusion to my personal hygiene. I'm beginning to smell myself and I guess you're right. I do stink. When

I saw Skilling I asked him if you and I could go to town for the day and he said to ask the Old Man. So I just told him we were going anyhow in case anybody asks where we are. Want to go, Bill? We're going to Cambridge and take a bath."

"You're going 'way to Cambridge to take a bath?" said Bill with surprise. "Hell, that's forty miles. There's a shower just a quarter of a mile from here, and if you have finally decided to take a bath I'll carry you there piggy-back."

"Thanks, just the same, Gargantua," answered Crolley sarcastically. "But it's just too damn cold for me. I'm going in town where I can get some warm water and a little privacy."

"How're you going to get there?" asked Bill.

"Well, it just so happens that they're sending a weapons carrier over to a fighter group right outside Cambridge to pick up some supplies of some kind," replied Crolley.

"How you goin' to get back?" asked Canyon.

"I should worry about that now," said Crolley. "We'll find a way tonight."

"We think we ought to take a chance, Dick?" queried McDevin. "I'd hate like hell to get stuck there all night. You know they could decide to fly us tomorrow. It's happened before on stand-down days. We could get in a hell of a lot of trouble."

"No guts," commented Crolley simply.

"It's not that," protested McDevin. "It's just common sense."

"To hell with common sense," countered Crolley. "What would they do to us, anyhow? They're too damned short on crews to do anything drastic. They need us more than we need them."

"They could fine you and give you an official reprimand," ventured Canyon.

"Possibly, but not likely," said Crolley. "Come on, McDevin, don't be chicken. The transportation leaves at ten-thirty."

"I'll go on one condition," said McDevin. "That we come back this afternoon and not wait until the last minute."

And so it happened. At ten-thirty McDevin and Crolley were bouncing through the English countryside along narrow roads toward Cambridge. They caught a shuttle truck from the fighter group just outside Cambridge into town and went directly to the Red Cross Officers' Club. They climbed the stairs to their rooms, dallied through a luxurious hot bath, and loafed about for almost two hours. It was nearly four o'clock.

"It's about time to head back, Dick," said McDevin. "I think we'd better start going."

Crolley was standing by the window. "It's raining like hell, Mike. We'll get soaked to the skin if we try to leave now. Let's wait for it to let up and call Linda and Doris."

"Let's just wait for it to let up," said McDevin dubiously. "I don't want to get involved with a bunch of dames. It's not fair to Katherine."

"Jeezis, look who's talking," said Crolley, registering genuine surprise. "Why the sudden change of heart?"

"It's not exactly a change of heart, Dick," said Mike. "I just got to thinking this morning. Just because I'm flying combat doesn't give me any excuse to be unfaithful to her. I know damn well she's being faithful to me."

'How do you know?" asked Crolley seriously.

"I just do," asserted McDevin. "I've known her for a long time. She's not the kind of person who would violate marriage vows. And besides, she's got a helluva high moral standard. She wouldn't carry on promiscuously under any circumstances."

"I guess you're right," said Crolley, "but look at it this way. You're a man and she's a woman. To my way of thinking, that makes a difference. I'm not saying that it's right to go out and whore around, but I don't think it's as bad for a man as for a woman. They have a whole lot more to lose and it cheapens them, whereas a man can get away with it."

"No, Crolley," said McDevin shaking his head. "Man and woman are equal in the sight of God, and it's just as much of a sin in His eyes for a man to commit adultery as for a woman."

"I'm not talking about what is a sin and what isn't a sin," replied Crolley. "I'm talking about human beings in our modern society. The way I look at it, the man has been provided with the initial desire. What I mean is, a man just naturally wants to have sexual relations—and a woman does, too, but they're not so pronounced. The male does the chasing, and the woman has to be worked up—unless she's a nymphomaniac. I'm not so naive as to think that a woman doesn't need a man. I've known a lot of old bitches that trip you and beat you to the ground. But most of them wouldn't actually go out and look for lovin'. They wait for somebody to offer it to them and make them want it."

"I agree with you partially," retorted McDevin. "But damned

65

if I don't believe the desire is almost equal. I realize a man is more liable to take the initiative, but if a woman wants to be pushed over, all she has to do is just to throw a hint, like standing on a corner, or going in a bar, waiting to be picked up. It's all in the way you think, Dick, and the kind of a man you are. If you're weak and you want to get laid and you're over here in combat, you can always justify it in your own mind by telling yourself that these are difficult times and you're not emotionally stable. You can always say, 'If I were home I wouldn't do this, but I'm over here and I can't help myself.' But, damn it, I *can* help myself. I don't think I'd ever become so overwrought by combat or anything else that I would lose my sense of moral responsibility. I can't say that I won't lay some babe while I'm over here. Hell, I might do it within the next hour or two, but, if I do, I'll know that I'm wrong, and I won't try to salve my conscience with any sort of justification."

"You're nuts, Mike," said Crolley. "You're looking at this thing ass backwards. Don't be so goddamn noble, sonny."

"Maybe I am nuts, Dick, but that's my philosophy, anyhow."

"I know how you can find out if you really feel the way you think you do, instead of just saying you feel the way you *believe* you should feel."

"How?" asked McDevin.

"Well, the next time you sleep with a strange dame, Mike, sit down and write Katherine a letter and say, 'Darling, I just got fixed up. I know I did wrong, and I'm sorry. I don't deserve to be forgiven.' "

"I agree with you, Dick," said McDevin with a sigh. "That's the acid test, all right, and I'll be damned if I'd ever write anything like that to Katherine. Hell, it would break her heart! She thinks I'm the finest guy in the world and I'm not going to do anything to disappoint her."

"That's all I wanted to know, Mike," said Crolley with some elation. "If you haven't guts enough to tell her, your long spiel about being so noble and your 'what's good for the goose is good for the gander' line is a bunch of stuff. You're a scalawag just like I am. Your only trouble is that your conscience is beginning to hurt you a little bit. Now, what do you say? Forget this goddamn foolishness and let's call Linda and Doris."

"Let's don't and say we did," said McDevin. But already

66

Crolley was at the telephone, trying to find Doris's number in the directory.

"Hell, she hasn't got a phone," said Crolley. "What was Linda's last name?"

"Chambers," said McDevin, "and she lives at Causewayside."

Crolley looked up at McDevin quickly and a sly grin crossed his face. "Old nobility himself," he chided, and laughed.

"All right, all right, so I got hot pants. What if I have? You yourself said it was all right, so quit rubbing it in. I still say it's wrong. I just haven't got guts enough to keep from doing it. You found her number yet?"

"Yeah, you want me to dial it?"

"Never mind, lover boy, I can take care of my own babes. I'll call her myself." He dialed Linda's number and hummed as he waited for an answer. "Hello, Linda? How are you today? . . . This is Mike McDevin. Don't you remember me? You were out to our base last week. . . . Don't get coy with me, sweetheart, I'm the guy you tried to make in the annex. . . . Okay, I'm sorry; I was just trying to be friendly. I didn't mean to insult you. Am I forgiven? . . . Dick and I had the day off so we thought we'd run in here to get a hot bath for a change. . . . Sure, I bathe every day but I get tired of that cold water. By the way, what are you doing at home this time of day, anyhow? . . . Oh, you told your supervisor you were ill. Winston Churchill wouldn't like that if he knew. . . . No, I wouldn't think of telling him, but next time I see you, you'd better be very nice to me or I'll call Winnie and give him the ungarbled word. . . . Don't be silly, I was only kidding. You have to be a general before Churchill will even talk to you. But you'd better watch out. They might promote me any day. . . . What do you mean I wouldn't even make a good sergeant in the RAF? I'd certainly like to see you. . . . No, I'm sorry we can't come for tea, we've got to get back to the base right away. . . . You say Doris is there? Just a minute. Hold the phone. . . ."

At the mention of Doris's name Crolley gesticulated wildly, trying to attract McDevin's attention. He said in a stage whisper, "Don't be a damn fool, Mike. It'll only take a minute."

"Damn it, Dick," said McDevin irritably. "If we go out there, you know as well as I do that we'll stay and we'll never get back to the squadron. I don't feel like getting court-martialed over a woman."

"Be reasonable, Mike. We'll check out here and catch a cab over to her apartment. We can hello and leave. Besides, maybe they can give us a lead on transportation back to the group."

"Okay, little bastard," conceded McDevin, "but do I have your word that we'll stay just a minute?"

"Yeah, yeah, sure," answered Crolley. "Just go ahead and tell her before she changes her mind."

"Hello, Linda. . . . Dick and I will catch a cab out there, but we can only stay a minute. Is Causewayside right? . . . Okay, darling. We'll see you in fifteen minutes. Bye, bye."

Causewayside was not a street but a huge apartment building. McDevin found the apartment number in the building directory, and Linda herself answered his ring.

"So glad to see you, Lieutenant," she said with feeling. "Oh! you're all wet!"

"How did you mean that?" smiled McDevin.

"Silly," scolded Linda. "I mean you're dripping. Did you walk in the rain?"

"No," answered McDevin, "but we had to wait awhile for a cab."

"Well, come in and take off those wet things, the both of you. Doris is in the kitchen, fixing tea."

"Thank you," said McDevin. "Come on, Dick. Seems like every time you see a woman you get tongue-tied."

"That's it," said Crolley. "Build me up." And the two went inside and removed their blouses while Linda made her way to the kitchen.

"Now remember, Dick," warned McDevin, while Linda was out of earshot, "we're only going to stay a minute. Don't get any bright ideas about sticking around here. The Old Man has probably got the whole M. P. squadron out looking for us already."

"You worry too much, McDevin," said Crolley with a laugh.

Doris came in laden with the tea tray. Linda followed in her wake. "Hello, Dick, darling!" gushed Doris. "I didn't think you'd ever come to see me after I deserted you the other night. Really, I'm quite sorry, but actually you were a bit fresh, you know, and I didn't relish being made love to on potato sacks. Besides you were getting quite drunk. Honestly."

"Whoa, slow down," said Crolley. "All is forgiven. Besides I deserved to be deserted, the way I was acting."

"That's not what you told me," interjected McDevin.

"Shut up, Mike, or I'll crown you with this teapot," cautioned Crolley.

"Are you two mates?" asked Linda.

"No, we're both boys," said Crolley innocently.

"I should have known," said Linda. "You're just over here, aren't you? I believe you Americans call it 'buddies.' What I mean is, are you always together?"

"Most of the time," answered McDevin. "I can't get rid of him so I put up with him."

"Oh, now, you don't mean that," said Doris.

"Definitely," said McDevin. "He's just like glue."

"In a pig's eye," said Crolley.

"I'm sure you boys didn't come here to fight," said Linda.

"No, you're right, sweetheart," informed McDevin. "We've got to get back to our group, anyhow, so there's no use wasting time making wisecracks."

"Say," said Crolley, "can you girls give us some idea of how to get transportation back to the base? We're too late to catch the train and I don't even know where the road is to start hitch-hiking."

"You're at Lavenham, aren't you?" asked Doris. "And that's just a short distance from Sudbury. There's a shuttle that leaves here around eleven o'clock from the Red Cross Club down town. It goes through Sudbury, I know, because I have a friend from there, a Lieutenant Ramey, who visits me occasionally, and he always uses it as transport back to his base. It's rather quick, too, he says. It only takes a couple of hours."

"What a break," said Crolley. "It's only five now. That gives us six hours."

"Now, listen, Dick," admonished McDevin. "I don't think we ought to take a chance."

"Oh, for God's sake, Mike, be sensible. I told Skilling we were going, and Canyon knows where we are. We'll be home by one o'clock in the morning."

"Well, all right," said McDevin, "but it's against my better judgment. Linda, how about going out to dinner with me and maybe we can take in a movie?"

"I have no objection if Doris hasn't," replied Linda. "I'm so glad you came, and I would enjoy an evening out. How about it, Doris, shall we go?"

"I should go home and change," said Doris. "I really can't appear in public like this."

"Well, I'll tell you what we'll do," said Crolley. "I'll take you home to change and then we'll go out and do what we want to and I can meet McDevin on the truck. Linda can tell him where it leaves from."

"Obviously, you are trying to separate us," said Doris with disdain. "I assure you if you attempt to seduce me again, tonight, I'll leave you straightway, like I did last time."

"Oh, go on, Doris," said Linda. "You can take care of yourself. Besides, I'd like to be alone with Mike."

"Oh, I say, Linda," said Doris. "You are being rather obvious."

"Of course not," said Linda. "It's just that I treated him rather shabbily when I saw him last, and I'd like an opportunity to show him that I'm not a heartless creature after all."

McDevin's heart pounded. Linda had cast the bait. It was up to McDevin to accept or reject it. His decision had to be quick because once he was alone with Linda, he thought he would go all the way. His better judgment told him to leave, but his passion was relentless and surged ever onward, completely conquering reason.

Crolley on the other hand had made up his mind that he was going to do his best to sleep with Doris that night. He was prone to cross his bridges when he came to them, never before. The thought of the chase intrigued him, and, at the moment, being in bed with Doris Errington was his fondest desire. Combat, his squadron, the group, flying, the Luftwaffe, and a sense of moral responsibility were all completely obliterated by insidious sexual desire. He didn't care if he was late. As a matter of fact, he didn't give a damn. All he wanted was Doris Errington, not as a woman, but as an outlet for his passion. Once he had committed his violation, in those fleeting seconds of regret that follow clandestine copulation, he would abhor Doris Errington, he would despise her and hate her very guts. She would have been but a vehicle of relief, and once she had provided such relief, she was of no concern to him until he again desired her body. His desire might return an hour later, but until that time he would loathe her. Then he would worry about returning to his squadron, then he would think about combat, the Luftwaffe, his group, and his fears of life and death.

"I'll be a perfect gentleman," lied Crolley to Doris. "Let's leave these two lovebirds alone. I'll take you home and then wherever you would like to go. After all, I couldn't do much towards seducing you. I have no room and it's light until nearly eleven o'clock. So I couldn't very well make love to you in the park or on somebody's lawn."

"All right," said Doris, "but I warn you, if you violate my trust just once more, I shall promise never to see you again."

But in her own mind Doris Errington was well aware that Crolley was going to attempt to seduce her for all he was worth that night. She expected it. If he didn't she would be disappointed. As a matter of fact, she knew that she would give in and her only worry was whether she could control herself long enough to make a good appearance. She thought she could fool Dick into thinking that if he seduced her it was because she was unable to prevent it, and that as soon as it was done she wanted him to feel as though he had irreverently trespassed on her chastity, that his act had been profane, that he had transgressed her set of moral laws. She wanted him to feel that he had abused her and defiled her body. She wanted to enjoy the ecstasy of uniting in sexual intercourse, but she wanted all the blame to rest upon the man. She wanted him to feel a hurt; she wanted his conscience to tell him that he had ravished her.

Crolley called a taxi and left Linda and McDevin alone.

"I'll see you at eleven, Mike," said Dick, as he departed.

"Just don't be late," admonished McDevin. "Make damn sure that you're there. Don't let your heart run away with your head."

Linda gazed at McDevin's back as he stood by the window, smoking a cigarette. She had a genuine desire to be alone with McDevin. Unlike Doris Errington, she had no thought of being seduced yet. She knew McDevin would try, but she also knew that he would be reluctant in his attempt, and if she rebuffed him at the outset, he would discontinue his efforts and content himself with conversation and tobacco until time to leave. Rather, she would yield just enough to egg him on, to prevent him from giving up the chase. She would encourage his passion slowly. She would tease this man just enough to insure his coming back, al-

71

though he would fail to make the grade this time—next time maybe yes. She looked hungrily at his long slim body, his well-proportioned head, and his handsomely formed shoulders. She wanted this man.

"Well, Linda," said McDevin, turning from the window, "what would you like to do? It has stopped raining and the sun is beginning to shine through."

"Oh, I don't care," answered Linda. "It's too early for dinner and it's stuffy in here. I'd like to go for a walk, if you don't mind."

"Not at all," said McDevin. "I'd like to see a bit of Cambridge. I've heard so much about it. By the way, is that a park in front of the house or just a wide expanse of lawn?"

"It's a park, really," said Linda. "Not a very pretty one, though. I'll show you around it. Are you ready?"

"I'll get my blouse. By the way, Linda, where's your mother?"

"Oh, she went to London this morning. She'll be back on the late train," answered Linda. Then after a pause she said, "Oh, I say, Mike, be a good chappy and don't start that again, just because we're alone."

"I didn't mean it that way," answered McDevin. "I simply wanted to meet her."

"Oh, how nice," said Linda. "That was very thoughtful of you."

McDevin put on his blouse while Linda fetched a coat. She brought it back and handed it to McDevin who held it up for her to slip into. He watched her graceful arms and beautiful fingers, as she lifted her hair from under the coat's collar. His eyes wandered down her slim body which was vibrant, even through the coat, and feasted on her trim angles and shapely legs. She turned around suddenly and planted moist lips on his, then rubbed her cheek on his jaw and said, "I do like you, Mike, really I do. Please don't think me brazen. I know we've only just met, but, dash it all, I've got a crush on you, a bad one."

. Mike pulled away in surprise and looked deep in her azure eyes. "Linda," he stammered, "I hate to be corny, but this is so sudden. I mean it. I should have told you that night at the club—I—I'm married, Linda, and I've got a little girl, a beautiful little tyke, just a year and a half old."

"I knew you were married, Mike," replied Linda. "Your wedding band gave you away. I know you think I'm terrible, but I didn't mean that I loved you. I just have a crush on you, much like a schoolgirl."

"I'm in love with my wife, Linda," said McDevin. "I shouldn't be here at all, but I was weak and let Dick talk me into it."

"Oh, well, you're here and there's no harm done. Shall we go for our walk?" She pulled away and walked toward the door.

"Before you go, Linda," said McDevin, "I'd like to say that I'm sorry for making advances toward you the other night. I guess I should say that I'm ashamed of myself. I'm ashamed because I shouldn't even think of doing such a thing when I'm married."

"I understand," whispered Linda, as he moved closer to her. Then she said brightly, "Come along, chappy, let's visit the park. Then I'll show you the chapel at the university." She opened the door.

McDevin guided her down the stairs and into the wet street. The air was fresh and clean after the rain, and the sunshine cast gaiety over the green lawns.

Meanwhile, Crolley and his companion had reached Doris's apartment.

"Would you mix some spirits while I change?" asked Doris. "You'll find the Scotch in the cabinet below the sink and there's splash on the floor at the end of the counter. I'll only be a minute."

"Take your time," said Crolley, "and I'll build us a couple of 'doozies.'" He made his way toward the kitchen which was in the rear of the apartment. It was well-kept and modern. The Scotch and soda were where Doris said they would be and Crolley got down two glasses from the pantry. He sampled the Scotch before he made the highballs. He carried the glasses back into the living room and placed them on the mantel above the fireplace. Doris entered almost immediately from the bedroom. She was wearing a thin negligée and Dick could tell without a second look that except for a pair of toeless shoes, she was clad in nothing else. She flung herself down on the divan, crossing two beautiful legs and allowing her negligée to slip loosely away from creamy-white knees. The bodice of her robe draped dangerously from her bosom.

"I thought I'd have my drink before I dress," said Doris, her eyes limpid and innocent.

"Of course," said Crolley. "That's a beautiful gown."

Doris fluttered her eyelids coyly and said softly, "Thank you." She lifted her glass. "I propose a toast, Dick, a toast to you. May you have success in all your endeavors and may you come through the war safely." She sipped ever so lightly and stared with wide eyes at Crolley from over her glass.

"Now it's my turn, Doris. I drink to you, a beautiful woman. There's nothing in this world quite so beautiful as a beautiful woman."

"You flatter me, Dick. What would you like to do tonight?"

"Whatever you like, dear," he answered, and his hand sought hers.

"I'm afraid Cambridge is pretty dead these days. The publicans have such a limited supply of beverages, what with the war and all. There is one place we could go, however. It's a very secluded little restaurant near the university. The proprietor is a friend of mine and I'm sure just this once he could give us some special food—then we could come back here. If you'd care to buy a bottle, we could have some more drinks."

Crolley readily consented to this, for the chase was on.

"I hope you don't think me inhospitable when I ask you to buy a bottle," said Doris, "but I don't make a great deal of money and it's almost impossible to buy Scotch except through the black market. It costs four pounds there."

"I'll be more than happy to supply the booze," said Crolley, quickly eager to please his quarry. The way he felt then, he would have brought a whole damn case. He reached over and kissed her lightly on the ear and then drew her close to him. She raised her lips and he kissed them hotly. She shuddered.

"You do make love beautifully, Dick," she cooed. "Kiss me again."

Crolley was almost violent in his response. He embraced her hungrily and his hand invaded her bosom. She yielded momentarily and then pushed him away. She jumped to her feet and said indignantly, "I asked you simply to kiss me. I didn't give you license to get fresh. You promised to be a gentleman you know."

Crolley apologized, uncertain whether she was honest in her indignation or simply putting on a front for the sake of appearance. He decided on the latter. He reasoned that if she weren't welcoming his advances, she wouldn't have shown herself clad only in a negligée nor flaunted her legs and breasts. He decided

74

wisely to forego any further display of passion until they returned to her flat, after dinner. Doris retired to her bedroom to dress, and Crolley finished his drink.

McDevin and Linda were walking, arm in arm, around the large expanse of lawn in front of Causewayside. They had explored all the paths and had discussed each other completely. As they approached an air raid shelter, Linda said, "I'm tired, Mike. Let's sit down and rest here," and she led the way inside the shelter. There were benches along the sides and it was dark and musty. "There's an old couch right over there," she said. "Mother and I brought it down here during the blitz."

She sat down heavily and sighed deeply, pulling McDevin close by her side. "I'm a hussy, Mike," Linda confessed. "I lured you in here to make love to me," and she pulled him close to her and kissed him lightly on the mouth. Then she leaned back on the couch in a semi-reclining position. McDevin followed the lead. "You can have me if you want me, Mike," she whispered softly, "but I beg of you, please don't try." McDevin was silent.

At a quarter of eleven, Linda and McDevin emerged from the air raid shelter and hurried toward the Red Cross Club.

"I can make it if I run," said McDevin. "I think I know the way. I got my bearings when the cab brought us up here. There's no need for you to come along."

"Yes, I am rather tired," said Linda. "Just follow this road all the way; bear left and you can't miss it. You will come and see me again, won't you, Mike?"

"Yes, of course," he responded. "I should get three days leave in a couple of weeks and I'll visit you then."

"Call me before you come," said Linda. "You have my number."

McDevin was at the Red Cross Club in five minutes. Crolley was there when he arrived.

"Where are the trucks?" asked McDevin.

"There aren't any," said Crolley, despondent. "It's a shuttle from Ipswitch and only runs on special occasions, like any other night but tonight."

"Goddamn it, I knew I shouldn't have listened to you," cursed McDevin. "How in the hell are we going to get back?"

"Don't get your bowels in an uproar, sonny boy. We hitch-hike.

I've already called a cab. He can take us to the edge of town on the main road and the first GI truck that comes along, we hop it."

McDevin was disgruntled. A quarter of an hour later they were outside Cambridge, standing forlornly on the road leading to Bury St. Edmunds.

"While we're waiting, we might just as well talk shop," said McDevin. "Did you get your ashes hauled?"

"Yeah," responded Crolley. "Twice. It was a beautiful job both times."

"Did she give you much trouble?"

"Nope, same old line. 'I've only done this once before. Please don't. If I let you, I'll hate myself.' The usual stuff. But she sure knew her business How'd you do, Mike?"

"No soap."

"Come on, buddy, this is Crolley you're talking to. You can tell all to me."

"No, I mean it. I could have, but I didn't."

"What's the matter with you, anyhow?"

"Nothing, I just couldn't bring myself to it."

The two were silent. Darkness came upon them suddenly and there was no sign of transportation. It was eleven-thirty when a huge, five-ton GI truck came lumbering slowly down the road. McDevin and Crolley flagged it down and asked the driver if they could ride along. The truck took them as far as Bury St. Edmunds which was still eight miles from the base. Just outside of town the two of them, in a vile mood and passing nasty remarks back and forth, hailed a jeep that was running angrily down the road in the right direction. It was occupied by a lone GI and for the small monetary consideration of one pound apiece he took them to their base. They showed the guard at the gate their AGO cards and walked the half mile to Hut Thirteen. They heard the roar of airplane engines on the line as the crew chiefs accomplished their pre-flights.

"What time is it, Dick?" asked McDevin.

"It's one-thirty. I just looked at my watch at the gate."

"Jeezis, I'm glad we don't have to fly today," said McDevin. "I'm dead tired."

"So am I," said Crolley. "I'm going to sleep until noon, if they'll let me."

They walked into Hut Thirteen and stopped abruptly inside the door. The light was on and Canyon was in the process of putting on his flying suit.

"You mean? . . ." asked Crolley in desperation, leaving the rest of the sentence understood.

Canyon laughed. "Yeah, 'I mean,' buddy. It's a maximum effort today. Light bomb load. The tanks are topped off and everybody flies, including Crolley and McDevin."

"Oh, hell," lamented McDevin. "Crolley, I'm never going to listen to you again as long as I live."

CHAPTER

6

T HE DAYS PASSED AND MC DEVIN, CROLLEY AND CANYON GREW older and older as the disheveling effects of combat began to wear upon them. Because of the great number of losses, it was difficult for the group commander to garner enough crews to put his missions in the air. As a result, few were allowed to go on pass. McDevin, Crolley and Canyon made occasional trips to nearby Bury St. Edmunds, visiting the Red Cross Officers' Club to bathe. On days when they were guaranteed immunity from availability for the next day's missions, they would venture into town and remain all night. On afternoons when they stood down and had completed their training schedule, they walked the two miles to Lavenham and visited Robbin's pub.

Robbin was huge and jovial and wore a small goatee. He liked the Americans and, unlike other pub keepers, he always kept plenty of cold ale, and sometimes even had Scotch. He collected antique weapons and other military accouterment of bygone years. He listened to the boys' troubles, if they had any, and if they didn't, he would tell them a few of his own.

Once in ahwile McDevin and Crolley would go to Cambridge for the night, to see Linda and Doris. McDevin was becoming fonder by the day of Linda. He recognized this and, because of a deep-seated sense of moral responsibility, he tried to stay away from her as much as he could. Left to his own devices, he could have exercised his will power and never have seen her again. But Crolley's maddened, increased desire for Doris Errington lured them both to Causewayside. Linda wrote nearly every day, nice chatty letters, not saying much except what was between the lines. McDevin suspected that Linda's feeling for him was something more than a schoolgirl's crush. But he never actually knew, and he was afraid to say anything to her for fear it was true.

One night after mess, Crolley and McDevin bellied up to the bar at the Officers' Club and ordered Scotch and soda. They were on their fourth when a tall lieutenant, cigarette in mouth, walked up beside them and ordered a pint of beer. Feeling convivial and a bit gay, McDevin turned to the newcomer and said, "Come, come, man, even my friend Crolley here wouldn't drink that stuff. It'll poison you."

"Oh, it's all right for a change," answered the lieutenant.

"By the way," said McDevin, "this is Lieutenant Crolley and my name is Mike McDevin. I've seen you around, but I don't know your name."

The tall lieutenant coughed, then answered, "My name is Lang," and he coughed again.

"That's a pretty bad cough you have there, Lang," said Crolley. "This damn English weather won't do it any good."

"No, I've had this goddamned thing for months," said Lang. "I can't seem to get rid of it. I haven't got a cold and Doc Lerdner can't find anything wrong with me." He paused momentarily, then said suddenly, "Say, McDevin, I've seen you down at communion in the morning before missions, but I never see you at mass."

"You know, it's funny I haven't met you before," said McDevin. "You're in the 838th, aren't you?"

"Yes, I fly with Les Gotland," answered Lang. "But I stick pretty close to the hut when we're not flying."

"Yeah, Dick and I do our drinking at home, too," said McDevin. "You'd better have some liquor instead of that stuff you're drinking." And then, calling to the bartender, he ordered, "Give us three double Scotch and sodas, Jimmy." After reconsideration, he added, nodding to Lang, "Make his a triple—he's behind."

"Holy Christ," said Lang. "Are you trying to get me stewed?"

"Why not?" asked Crolley. "We're stood down again tomorrow. Just as well we got drunk tonight. It's a lot of fun. This is our fifth drink already. Pretty soon we'll start telling stories, then McDevin will beat the hell out of the piano and we'll all sing dirty songs."

"Come on, let's drink up," said McDevin. "The bar closes in three hours."

"You're too much for me," said Lang.

"What's your first name?" asked Crolley.

"George," answered the lieutenant, as though he were confessing something unpleasant. He coughed spasmodically.

"That settles it," said McDevin. "From now on we call you 'The Lung.'"

"Rosiland would love that." said the newly tagged lieutenant.

"What's that?" asked Crolley.

"My wife," answered The Lung.

"Another fool," said Crolley. "You guys who get married are out of your heads. Now, take Michael Patrick here. He's got a wife named Katherine and he's got a gal in Cambridge named Linda. Brother, is she hot after his body! But he won't lay her because he says, 'It isn't fair to Katherine.' Now me, I'm not married and I got a girl in Cambridge named Doris who I sleep with regularly. McDevin's gettin' overweight carrying around all those ashes he ought to have hauled."

"Nothing's sacred to you, is it, you little bastard" said McDevin, with just the slightest irritation. "At least I don't have to worry about venereal disease. That's more than you can say."

"Oh, I don't know," said Crolley. "Doc Lerdner takes good care of me. Besides, the way I make love with her, she doesn't want anybody but me."

"What do you think of a guy like that?" asked McDevin.

"Let's have another drink," answered The Lung. The effect of the triple shot was beginning to tell.

"Pregnant idea," said Crolley with ardor. "Hey, Jimmy, three doubles and go easy on the soda. It's your turn to pay, Mike."

"Hell, I paid for the last two."

"Yeah, but you owe me three from last night."

"Jeezis, what a cheap skate. You get flying pay just like I do. Hell, I've never seen a navigator yet that wasn't a cheap skate."

"I'll be damned if I don't agree with you," said Lang. "Our navigator is the tightest guy in the group."

"What's your rating, Lung?" asked Crolley.

The Lung coughed, unzipped his field jacket and displayed his wings.

"Another bomb aimer," said McDevin, shaking The Lung's hand vigorously.

"Too bad," murmured Crolley.

"Oh, shut up, you goddamn star gazer," said McDevin. Then turning to Lang he said, "Disappointing, isn't it?"

"Oh, I don't care," answered The Lung. "What the hell's the difference? You get shot at one way or the other. I got washed out of pilots' school in 1942 so I went on to bombardier school."

"What was the matter?" asked McDevin.

"Christ, I couldn't fly a kite," complained The Lung.

"Well, at least he's honest," interposed Crolley. "A bombardier's nothing more than a pilot with his brains knocked out, anyhow."

"Pay for the drinks," said McDevin. "Then go flush yourself down a toilet."

After another hour of aimless bickering about the relative merits of bombardiers and navigators, and having drunk several more double Scotch and sodas, the three repaired to an ancient, upright piano and McDevin began to render a few of the more risqué, traditional songs of the service. At eleven o'clock the bar closed and when the bartenders had retired for the evening, McDevin picked a lock on the club's storeroom door and he and Crolley lugged out a keg of beer. There were some twenty officers left in the club and by midnight the keg was dry.

Midway through the beer-bust, The Lung found his way to the rear of the piano and lay down with six mugs of beer by his side. Between coughing spasms, he sang over and over again, in that voice peculiar to drunks, loud and with no resemblance to melody, "She was only a caretaker's daughter, but, oh, how she took care of me."

Crolley made several trips back and forth to the latrine but failed to return from his last journey. McDevin set out to find him. Searching the club thoroughly, and nearly getting lost himself, he found Crolley in the kitchen, placidly munching dry cereal.

"What in the hell you doin', you sloppy old drunk?" asked McDevin thickly.

"I'm hungry," answered Crolley, spewing corn flakes as he spoke.

"Why didn't you cook some eggs or something?"

"No hens."

"Got any more corn flakes?" asked McDevin.

"I'm sitting on a whole goddamn case."

"What are you doin' back here, anyhow?" asked McDevin, hiccoughing violently.

"I've been hunting for those goddamn potato sacks," and Dick munched contentedly.

"Got any more corn flakes?" asked McDevin again.

"I'm sittin' on a whole goddamn case of them."

"Did you say that before?"

"I'm too drunk to remember. These corn flakes sure cut up your stomach," lamented Crolley.

"Why don't you chew them?"

"I just kinda gum 'em."

"Don't your gums get sore?"

"I don't have to pay the dentist here so I should worry. Besides, what's a sore gum or two. Maybe they'll ground me for it. Blooding gums! Hell, I'll blood all over the squadron area. They wouldn't dare make me fly."

"How about lettin' me blood a little, too?" said McDevin. Then he exclaimed suddenly, "Say, let's be saboteurs. We'll feed everybody in the squadron corn flakes. Then they'll all blood at the gums. Then nobody can fly and we can all go to London."

"Seems to me," answered Crolley, "that it should be 'bleed' instead of 'blood.' "

"You and your bloody red tape. Get it? Ha, ha! Bloody red tape, ha!" He paused and then added solemnly, "Let's take the corn flakes with us."

"Wait'll I finish this box. Don't want to waste it, you know."

"Hell, that's a big box."

"I know it; my gums are blooding something fierce."

After considerably more of the same nonsensical banter, Crolley and McDevin carried away several large boxes of corn flakes. On the way to their hut Crolley asked McDevin, "Whatcha doin' with those corn flakes?"

McDevin, thoroughly drunk by now, looked from side to side and said quickly, "Sh, I'm blazin' a trail."

"What the hell for?"

"You heard about Gansel and Hetel, haven't you?"

"They put their finger in the dike or something, didn't they?"

"Naw, that was Little Boy Blue. Anyhow, Gansel and Hetel left a trail of crumbs when they went into the forest so they could find their way back again. That's what I'm doin'. I'm marking a trail so we can find our way back to the club again."

They walked on slowly. Crolley opened a box of corn flakes and began skipping down the road, singing, "Here we go gathering nuts in May," throwing corn flakes from side to side. McDevin followed suit.

Upon reaching the doorway of their hut, McDevin said thickly,

"You know, Dick, somethin's missin'. We left somethin' at the club. Check all your belongings."

"Hell, I know what it is!" said Crolley, triumphantly, finding it difficult to stand, "The Lung."

"Shall we just leave him there?" asked McDevin.

"He might catch cold," said Crolley. "Besides, the last time I saw him, he had a whole bunch of beer mugs—all full."

"I guess we'd better go get him," said McDevin. "Maybe he's got some left," and they hurried back to the club as fast as their wobbly legs would carry them.

The Lung was in deep repose behind the piano. He was in a state of semi-consciousness, but all his beer was gone. McDevin and Crolley had a long discussion as to what to do. There were three courses of action open, according to McDevin's logic. One, they could leave him there; two, they could prop him up in a chair; three, they could carry him home and put him to bed. Crolley, drunk as he was, recklessly suggested that they pick his pockets, but they wisely decided against it. Their final decision was to carry him home. Occasionally, The Lung would let out a few tuneless bars of *She was Only a Caretaker's Daughter* and then lapse back into silence. McDevin and Crolley labored carrying him home by his hands and feet with his buttocks dragging the ground. They laid him gently on the floor by Canyon's bed and, not bothering to remove his or their own clothes, they crawled happily into bed and fell into a deep alcoholic sleep.

* * *

At seven the next morning, Bill Canyon stretched lazily, yawned and sat up in bed. The English morning crept around the fringes of the blackout curtains and the dampness of the new-born day infiltrated through the numerous cracks of Hut Thirteen. He was startled by a movement from beside his bed, and it was then that he noticed the subtle indication of whiskey which hung heavily in the air. He jumped out of bed and switched on the light. The Lung's long, grotesque form was sprawled carelessly on the brown linoleum floor, his face a mask of serenity.

Canyon smiled, and there were sly crinkles at the corners of his eyes. He picked up the empty coal bucket and shovel and, raising them at arm's length, dropped them crashing to the floor. The Lung coughed and moved restlessly, as if searching for a

83

more comfortable position. McDevin and Crolley were silent in their beds. Having failed to wake the trio, Canyon dressed and left the hut. In a moment he was back, bringing with him Misch Hour, Doc Lerdner, and Willy Birtland, each with a coal pail and shovel in hand. At a given signal from Canyon they all began to beat rhythmically on their coal pails, singing: "Throw a nickel on the drum; Save another drunken bum; Hallelujah, Hallelujah, Throw a nickel on the drum and you'll be saved." Reaching the coda, they repeated.

McDevin was the first to respond. "Oh, God, get the hell out of here. We had a rough night."

Whereupon Canyon and his chorus repeated their song, beating all the harder on the coal pails. Crolley was next to be revived. "I'm going to shove those goddamn coal pails right where they hurt the most. Beat it, you bastards."

"Hey, come on, have a heart, will you?" pleaded McDevin. "It's no skin off your butt if we go out and have a good time. Let us die in peace."

The tormenting quartet laughed with great hilarity.

Willy Birtland said, "I haven't had so much fun since my sister caught her finger in the wringer."

"That ain't the way I heard it," said Misch Hour.

"I wish you guys were dead. On second thought, I wish I were dead," said McDevin.

"Who in the hell is that layin' on the floor?" asked Canyon.

"That's a refugee we brought home last night," said Mike. "He was homeless and friendless and didn't have a place to sleep."

"From the looks of things, he didn't need it," laughed Birtland.

"Why don't one of you guys wake him up?" asked Crolley.

"Maybe he's dead," said McDevin. "God, my head hurts."

Misch Hour bent over and shook The Lung violently. He muttered, almost inaudibly, "She was only a caretaker's daughter," and, sighing, went back to sleep.

After several attempts to arouse The Lung, including more beating of coal buckets (much to the chagrin of McDevin and Crolley), and the merciless yanking of several hairs from his Hitler-like mustache, the tormentors finally resorted to cold water. The Lung raised his head slowly from the floor. Squirting a small stream of water from between his teeth and mopping his brow with a shaky hand, he expelled several irreverent words.

Suddenly, he bolted upright and looked questioningly around through red, swollen eyes.

"Good morning, Lung," said McDevin, not bothering to move from his sack.

The Lung groaned. "How in the hell did I get here?" he muttered, as he gingerly rubbed the bruises wrought by the previous night's journey from the club. "I must have acted pretty bad last night."

"Disgracefully," admonished Crolley. "McDevin and I begged you not to do it, but you completely disregarded the advice of older and wiser heads."

"Humph," gargled The Lung. "The last thing I remember was you and McDevin singing 'Blood on the Highway and I Didn't Hear Nobody Pray, Brother.' McDevin was playing and you were keeping time by beating two beer mugs together."

"Strictly a figment of your drunken imagination," said Crolley.

"Don't pay any attention to the little roustabout, Lung," said McDevin. "He led us both astray last night. I suppose you know everybody here except Canyon. He's that ugly-looking abortion with the coal pail in his hand. He's obsessed with coal pails. Everytime Crolley and I tie one on, he has to beat coal pails."

"It's nothing more than you deserve," said Canyon. "Glad to know you, Lung. I've seen you around." He extended his hand.

The Lung coughed and attempted to arise but promptly sat down again. "Oh, I'm dyin'," he moaned. "Doc, fix me up. Somebody call the priest. I haven't got much longer." His face had a peculiar greenish hue. After a considerable struggle, he pulled himself up long enough to lay down on Canyon's bunk. "Come on, Doc," he pleaded. "Diagnose me or something."

Doc Lerdner, who had been enjoying the proceedings in silence, stepped over to The Lung's bedside and made a mock examination. "This is a very sad case, indeed," said the doctor, very professionally. "This man suffers from Adiadochocinesis," and he shook his head sadly from side to side.

"Is it serious?" asked The Lung. "Do you think you'll have to operate?"

"Possibly," mused the doctor. "But I think you can forego such a thing by clean living."

"Oh, I'm very clean, Doctor. What is this Adia-whatever-it-is? Do you think you can cure it?"

"I'm afraid you'll have it for the rest of your life," answered the doctor.

"Maybe I won't have to fly combat, huh?" said The Lung, brightening considerably.

"I told you not to drink so much," said Crolley, "but nobody ever listens to me."

"And what's more," said McDevin, "nobody ever will if I have anything to say about it. Your antics last night convinced me that you're ready for a Section Eight."

"We never section eight navigators," piped Hour. "When they get that way, we just make bombardiers out of them."

"Spoken like a gentleman and a scholar," said Crolley.

"Let's get back to me and my condition," said The Lung with concern. "Were you serious, Doc, about this Adiadocho stuff? I know the doctor back home said I shouldn't drink much at one time."

"I'm afraid I am serious," said Doc Lerdner, trying hard to keep a straight face. "Your case of Adiadochocinesis is acute."

The Lung closed his eyes and moaned, "Hell, I thought you were kidding at first."

Doc Lerdner began to laugh. He said, "Don't worry, Lung, all that's troubling you is a bad hangover." And he went on to explain, "Anyone who is unable to perform rapid alternating movements has Adiadochocinesis. And from the look of you, I don't think you can do it today. Of course, that's a pretty simple treatment of the subject, but I think you get the idea."

The Lung was visibly embarrassed and everyone in the hut snickered. "That was a dirty goddamn trick, Doc."

"I know," answered Doc Lerdner, still laughing, "but it was too good to pass up."

"Listen, sawbones," said The Lung, "if I didn't have Adiadochocinesis I'd pass you up with a good swift kick in the butt, doctor or no doctor."

Both Doc Lerdner and Misch Hour had derived considerable glee from the entire situation as had Willy Birtland, and the three departed with loud guffaws and last-minute tantalizing remarks directed at The Lung.

Crolley began squirming in his bed. "Something sure as hell scratches," he complained.

"Maybe you ought to take more baths," suggested Canyon.

"Hell, I'll scratch forever before I'll take another bath in that cold water." He arose from his bed and lighted a cigarette, still scratching violently. He began taking off all his clothes. Halfway through he stopped suddenly and exclaimed, "Corn flakes. Those goddamn corn flakes. I got 'em all over me." He shook each garment systematically and stripped down to his skin.

While he was in the midst of this, the door opened, and Captain Skillings walked in with a purposeful look on his face. "Now isn't this cozy," he said with a snicker. "Already I've caught the culprit," and he gazed meaningfully at the evidence of corn flakes on the floor. "It's a funny thing," he continued. "I was just talking to the club mess officer and he told me some sneaky little bastard got into his corn flakes last night and whoever it was left a trail from the club 'way down to Hut Thirteen. And he isn't very happy about it. You guys must have had a hell of a party."

"Yeah, some jag," answered McDevin. "Too bad about someone getting into the mess officer's corn flakes—just so they didn't get into his pants."

"And somebody stole a keg of beer, too, but they can't prove who did it."

Crolley and McDevin were silent.

"Well, you couldn't prove it by me," said The Lung. "I can't remember from nothing. Besides, I think I'm pregnant from the pains I'm having this morning."

Skilling laughed good-naturedly. "Well, I didn't come down here to raise hell with you boys. Rather I bring happy tidings. Since we got those new replacements, the Old Man has started to give leaves. Since you guys haven't had any yet, he's going to let you go first."

"Does that include me?" asked The Lung quickly.

"Hell, no," said Skilling. "We're never going to give you a pass. You're too goddamn ugly. As a matter of fact, we're going to let you fly tomorrow, George."

"If I'm not dead by then," lamented The Lung.

CHAPTER

7

A PASS TO LONDON WAS ONE OF THE BRIGHTER POINTS IN THE lives of combat crewmen in the Eighth Air Force during World War II. McDevin, Crolley, and Canyon had been in the Group two months and had flown eleven missions, but, because of the shortage of crews, this was their first chance for a pass to leave the base for any length of time. From the other members of their squadron, who were there before they had arrived, came glowing tales of hotel rooms with bathtubs and hot and cold running water, girls of unsavory reputation who were called "Piccadilly Commandos," and who populated Piccadilly Circus, T-bone steaks in black market restaurants, "bottle clubs" which sold Scotch whiskey for the equivalent of eighteen dollars in American money per fifth, a place called the "Windmill Theater" that boasted a great array of nude women, to say nothing of Westminster Abbey and its tomb of famous people, Hyde Park with its soapbox orators, the torture chambers of the Tower of London, Headquarters SHAEF and Eisenhower, Their Majesties the King and Queen of the British Empire, and Winston Churchill. These stories of their fellow officers', though fifty per cent recognizable exaggeration, had created an eager desire to visit this magnetic city on the Thames, which was the citadel of a people who once ruled the largest empire in the world.

McDevin, Crolley, and Canyon hurried through their ablutions, packed a musette bag apiece, and put on their best uniforms which had been carefully pressed and hung in storage for just such an occasion. They caught a truck to Long Melford, five miles away, and boarded a small passenger train for the three-hour ride to London. They thoughtfully had included a fifth of bourbon among their accouterment, to make the trip more enjoyable. They divided it equally among themselves and restrained their thirst so rigorously that the last drop was drained just as they pulled into Liverpool station. It was huge, smoky, and dark, and it teemed with hundreds of Americans who, like McDevin, Crolley, and

Canyon, were coming from various parts of England to spend three days of gaiety in London.

McDevin asked a nonedescript GI directions to the subway station, which would take them uptown. They had been apprised of a number of things by previous visitors and their procedure was pretty well in mind. When they reached the tube station, they purchased tickets from automatic vending machines and fought the crowd to the nearest departure dock. They made their way through a maze of tunnels and down the continuously moving escalators. They were caught in a mob of bodies and barely got aboard the subway train before it began whisking through the tube at seventy miles an hour toward the Marble Arch station, the trio's destination. There had been the usual banter and insults passed back and forth among the three, and the tempo of their garrulity increased as they neared their destination. At the Marble Arch station they debarked from the train and rode the escalators to the surface. Once outside, they were next door to the Cumberland Hotel, on Oxford Street, across from Hyde Park.

"So this is London," said McDevin.

"Yeah, this is London," answered Canyon. "But I suggest we go get our rooms. Skilling told me hotels were pretty crowded."

"Always the practical one," said Crolley. "Here we are gazing at famous Hyde Park on Oxford Street in London, a sight we thought we'd never see, and this yokel from Iowa right away wants to get down to business."

"Maybe so," answered Canyon, "but if we don't get a place to sleep, we'll have to stay up all night."

"A very profound observation," ventured Crolley. "How long did it take you to figure that one out?"

Canyon cuffed his companion playfully on the side of the head.

"What's all the fuss about?" said McDevin. "I thought you called the Cumberland for reservations."

"I did," said Canyon, "but you know how undependable these limeys are."

"Hell, I thought they were dependable," said Crolley. "At least they depend on Uncle Sam for everything. That's a joke in case your brain isn't fertile enough to catch it."

Amid laughter and prognostication of what the night would hold, the three made their way the short distance to the Cumberland Hotel. They were greeted cordially by the room clerk who was holding their reservations for them. As they were about to depart for their room, she called them back, and with a very pleasant smile asked, "What time shall I knock you up, gentlemen?"

"That's antithetical," said McDevin. "But I think I get the idea. So far as I'm concerned, you can do it now. I'd just as soon be pregnant by you as anybody."

"Oh, for God's sake, Mike," blushed Canyon.

The room clerk was visibly embarrassed. "Oh, I say, you are crude. But I should know about you Americans, by now. What I meant was, at what time do you wish to be called?"

"What is she, a call-house madam?" muttered Crolley under his breath.

"Oh, no particular time," answered McDevin. "We're here for a rest."

"Will you have breakfast in your rooms?" she asked, regaining her composure.

"I'm beginning to like London more every minute," said Crolley. "Sure we'll have it in bed, why not?"

"We stop serving at nine these days. The war you know," answered the room clerk.

"We'll be doing good if we get in by that time," answered McDevin. "We'll let you know later."

"I simply must know now," she said, somewhat irritated. "We have such a great number of people, you must cooperate. Actually."

"Okay, forget it. We'll eat when we get up. Thanks, anyhow," said McDevin.

They rode the elevator to the eighth floor and were led to their rooms by a disgruntled English counterpart of the American bellhop. The rooms were modern and luxurious with a bathroom and an enormous bathtub. Crolley and McDevin bunked together in number 801 and Canyon took a room down the hall. Canyon, being a little cross with McDevin's and Crolley's display of poor manners toward the room clerk, had gone to his room and said he would be down later, after he had had a bath.

Crolley flung his musette bag on the room's only armchair and plopped on the luxurious bed. He relaxed completely.

"Peel me a grape, Mike. Then run in three or four naked women. I'm ready."

"I'm sure glad I don't carry on," answered McDevin, who had already begun to undress. "Upright and upstanding, that's me. None of this illicit skullduggery for me."

"I didn't know skullduggery could be licit," answered Crolley.

"Listen, Webster," protested McDevin, "we're on pass and we're out to rest and have a good time. Let's make an agreement right here and now. Let's not ride each other about technicalities."

"Agreed," said Crolley. "But I still don't see how skullduggery can be licit, the word itself meaning . . ."

"Never mind, I know what it means. Now just shut the hell up," said McDevin. "I'll flip you to see who takes his bath first."

"You go ahead," yawned Crolley. "I'm just going to lay here and rest. Boy, I haven't lain on a bed like this since I left Springfield."

"I didn't know they had beds in Springfield," said McDevin from the bathroom, as he turned on the massive water faucets.

"Oh, we have beds all right," answered Crolley. "We just don't have enough to go around, so everybody doubles up. That's why we have so many kids in Springfield. And the more kids we have the more we have to double up, and the more we double up, the more kids we have . . ."

"All right, all right," broke in McDevin. "It's a vicious circle. You don't have to explain it. Boy this water feels good, and this tub is so goddamned big you can stretch all the way out."

"I'll bet you this bed feels better than your water," challenged Crolley.

"Let's desert," suggested McDevin. "They'd never find us in London. Gee, this tub is big. Reminds me of the one we had in our fraternity house. We use to mix 'turkey-wurkey' in it every year when we had our pirate dance."

"What the hell is 'turkey-wurkey'?" queried Crolley.

"It was a drink that separated the men from the boys," retorted McDevin. "Two gallons of wood alcohol, two fifths of gin, a fifth of rum and the juice of one lemon."

"What was the lemon for?" asked Crolley.

"We had a house rule against straight drinks."

"I should have known," said Crolley. "Any fraternity that would take you in is bound to have damn-fool rules. By the way, which one did you belong to?"

"Sigma Chi," answered McDevin proudly. "You know, 'The girl of my dreams is the sweetest girl.' "

"When are you going national?" asked Crolley.

"That does it," exploded McDevin in mock wrath. "You go to hell. Besides, what do you know about it? You don't even belong to a fraternity."

"Who the hell cares?" said Crolley. He paused, then added in sudden outrage, "When in the hell are you going to get out of that bathtub? You've been there for five minutes, already."

"I offered to flip you. Now you can just wait."

"Like hell I'll wait. . . ."

Just then Bill Canyon entered through the unlocked door. "Are you two jerks at it already? Don't you ever let up?"

"I was just ready to call you, Bill," said Crolley. "McDevin has been making indecent advances toward me."

"Don't you believe him, Bill," defended McDevin. "It was the other way around. You know that I am clean of mind and body."

"Well, let's hurry up and get started," said Canyon. "Hell, I've bathed and shaved already and even put on some sweet-smelling perfume."

Just then there was a knock at the door.

"Come in. It's your funeral," said Crolley. Canyon opened the door and in walked a pert little English maid, carrying an armful of towels. "I've brought some towels," she said, and there was a twinkle in her eyes.

"Thanks, sweetheart," said Crolley. "Just throw them anywhere. Lie down and tell me the story of your life."

She laid the towels down on a desk and said, with a toss of her head, "Oh, aren't you the one."

"I certainly am, baby," said Crolley, getting up from the bed.

"My God, Crolley," said Canyon. "You won't stop at anything, will you?"

"What's going on out there?" said McDevin's voice from the bathroom.

"A female just entered the room," answered Canyon, "and, as usual, Crolley has lost all sense of reason. Hey, where are you going, Dick?" But already Crolley was out of the room.

McDevin got out of the bathtub and dried his body vigorously with the huge Turkish bath towel. As he shaved, he discussed the evening's plans with Canyon. "Before we go any further," he said, "look in my musette bag and dig out that bottle. I gave old Doc Lerdner a snow job before we left and he gave me a fifth of bourbon. I'll take about four fingers in one of those water glasses."

Canyon poured drinks for the two of them and took McDevin's to him in the bathroom. They toasted each other and drank deeply.

"What in hell happened to Crolley?" asked McDevin.

"He followed the maid out in the hall. You know how Crolley is," answered Canyon.

"Know how he is?" exclaimed McDevin in alarm. "I'll say I know how he is. We'd better go find him before he gets in trouble. Remember how he chased that gal up and down the corridor in the Cornhusker Hotel in Lincoln? Now that the little bastard is overseas, you can't tell what he'll do," and McDevin ran to the bedroom and quickly slipped on his trousers. He followed Canyon out of the door. They went up and down each corridor, carefully checking all open doors and any nook that was large enough to hold a man and woman. Suddenly, from around the corner, came a squeal, and presently the body of a girl flashed past them on a dead run, with Crolley in close pursuit.

"We'll catch him on the next go around," cried McDevin. "We'll ambush him at the next corner."

"What if he catches up with her before then?" asked Bill. "He was gainin' on her when he ran past us."

"We sure as hell can't catch him if we follow them," said Mike. "Let's run around the opposite way."

"Let's just go back in the room and wait," said Canyon with disgust.

"Hell, we can't leave him to die," countered McDevin.

"Why not?" said Canyon. "He'd be better off than the way he is now."

"Maybe you're right," agreed Mike.

As he spoke, the muffled sound of running feet sounded in the carpeted corridor, and the maid, still squealing, with dress held high, came around the corner at increased velocity. McDevin and Canyon applied football tactics and flattened the oncoming Crolley just as he entered his pursuit curve. The maid disappeared from sight.

"Now, why in the hell did you want to do that," puffed Crolley.

93

"I just about had her in my grasp. I would have caught her if you had let us go around again."

"What good would it have done?" asked McDevin, getting to his feet and examining a bare toe which he had bruised in the scuffle. "If you'd done anything, it would have been rape."

"Like hell it would have," answered Crolley. "She was just playin' hard to get."

"I wouldn't *play* hard to get if I were a girl being chased by you," said Canyon. "I'd be hard to get, period. If this is an example of what the rest of our pass is going to be like, I'm going to quit here and now."

"You're just narrow-minded, Bill," said Crolley.

The three went back to McDevin's and Crolley's room. Looking back on the incident, McDevin and Canyon thought it rather funny and Crolley lamented the fact that his chase had been unrewarded.

Within an hour they were once again on Oxford Street.

"What'll we do now?" asked McDevin. "We've been waitin' for this for two months and now that we're here we haven't any idea of what we want to do."

"You know damn right well what we're going to do," said Crolley.

"I know," admitted McDevin, "but where are we going to find it?"

"On Piccadilly Circus," answered Canyon. "Where everybody else does. According to the poop the bellboy gave me, we catch the tube at Marble Arch and we can get off right at the Piccadilly Station."

McDevin, Crolley, and Canyon once again descended underground and boarded the subway. Ten minutes later they emerged on Piccadilly Circus. They were standing directly by the arches. To the left was the Regent Palace Hotel. To the extreme right was a hexagonal block which was the center of a round, open space from which radiated Regent Street, Shaftesbury Avenue, Coventry Street, and a number of others, including, of course, Piccadilly.

It was getting dusk and nocturnal adventurers were setting forth on their nightly excursions. McDevin, Crolley, and Canyon made their way across the street to the Regent Palace Hotel amongst thick crowds, mostly American GI's, English girls waiting for a good time, and opportunists seeking their fortune from the unsuspecting. Well-kept London taxis, resembling Model A Fords, scurried back and forth, their squeaky horns adding to the confusion of this London Times Square. A score of Military Police were busy admonishing and arresting GI offenders.

The entrance of the Regent Palace Hotel is at the very apex of the angle formed by the joining of two streets as they pour into Piccadilly Circus. There were hundreds of people in and around its doors. Young, well-dressed, attractive prostitutes peddled their wares. They came from the lowest slum-dwelling families to the upper middle class. They greedily had become members of the oldest and least-honored profession since the war had ripped into the economic vitals of England, causing hardships at every turn. These young ladies could labor in the war effort for five or six pounds a week, but it was much easier for them to sell their bodies and souls for five or ten pounds per night, according to their relative attractiveness, for three weeks out of each month. They fully realized that there would be a blot on their names for the rest of their lives, but that mattered little now, what with the German Blitz, rockets, and buzz-bombs. Many of them were married and had husbands with the British army or the RAF in various parts of the world. Unlike the Americans, the British did not practice a policy of rotation of troops.

Some of these promiscuous females had ignored their native countrymen in matrimony and had become the wives of unwise, war-hysterical American soldiers. They were nothing more than sex marriages on the part of the GIs and honeymoons were spent in beds and bars. To the women it was an additional source of income for, as the wives of American servicemen, they were eligible for the allotment furnished by a generous American Government to military dependents. They saw their American husbands but little for there was a war to be fought. When their spouses departed to engage the enemy in combat, they flocked to Piccadilly Circus and began engaging other Americans in bed. They even bragged to prospective customers that they were married to Americans, because they thought it enhanced their prestige—and for some strange reason it did. As a matter of fact, a great number of these girls who were not actually married, claimed that they were American war brides, to help business and to attach a premium to them as bed partners.

95

McDevin, Crolley, and Canyon, being officers, and therefore men of relative wealth compared with the enlisted men, were accosted by a number of these whores as they entered the outside lobby of the Regent Palace Hotel. They all talked at once, each claiming to be the finest lay in London, with a fine bed for the rest of the night and breakfast in the morning. Canyon strode into the hotel in disgust, while McDevin and Crolley looked over the lot carefully, turning several around and pinching their bodies indiscreetly, as if trying to decide which to take.

"I'm sorry," said Crolley to the girls, "but there's not one here who could stand the strain. My friend and I are looking for something special." And he turned and followed McDevin into the lobby, leaving a highly disgruntled group of women in his wake.

They joined Canyon near the desk and wandered back to one of the hotel's spacious dining rooms where they ordered dinner. They dawdled over wine and cigarettes, took advantage of the service, and when their food was served they gulped it with relish despite their caustic comments concerning its inadequacy. Crolley was most vehement in his criticism.

"For a hotel like this they certainly serve crappy food," he lamented. "I've had better meals in Joe's Diner back in Springfield at a third the price."

"They've got food in Springfield?" asked McDevin. "To listen to you talk, everybody exists on bourbon."

"We eat occasionally," answered Crolley, ignoring McDevin's innuendo. "We do it to show the rest of the country that we're democratic."

"What do you call these goddamn things that look like sausages?" asked Canyon.

"Sausages," said McDevin.

"Oh, aren't you cute," said Canyon.

"My mother thinks I'm pretty," said McDevin.

"They taste like they're made from sawdust," griped Crolley.

"Hell, they are," McDevin informed him. "I thought you knew that. There's such a meat shortage here that they've added some kind of a synthetic derived from wood. You should have ordered fish, like I did."

"It's not Friday," said Crolley.

"What the hell difference does that make? You're not Catholic. Let's order another drink."

96

Just then their waiter approached the table and asked, "Would you gentlemen mind sharing your table? We're very crowded. . . ."

"Male or female?" asked Crolley.

"Beg your pardon?" queried the waiter.

"With whom?" asked McDevin.

"Two American nurses, one a captain and another a lieutenant. They're most anxious to dine, but at the moment we're all filled up. They asked me if I would request that you share your table with them. They are perfectly willing to take care of their own note."

"Well, don't stand there like an idiot," said Crolley. "Bring 'em on." The waiter scurried away.

"What if they're pigs?" asked McDevin.

"We'll feed 'em slop," answered Crolley.

"You don't mean you're going to pay for this?" asked Canyon, who was prone toward frugality.

"Why not?" said Crolley. "It may pay off. Besides that, I'm a gentleman. If you think I'm going to let American womanhood flounder, you're badly mistaken. Besides, when you sleep with a nurse you know you're safe."

"Not always," said McDevin. "They're susceptible like anybody else."

"Well, even if you do get V.D.," answered Crolley, "you can always go back to them for the cure, and you never have to turn in on sick call. They furnish the penicillin—needle and all."

"One of you boys in trouble?" asked a rich, melodious voice. And there stood a blond lieutenant of the Army Nurses Corps, resplendent in her uniform. She was beautiful, as Army nurses go, with dark eyes, olive skin, sensuous lips, and a slightly Roman nose. Her body was well proportioned, though stocky, and her appearance evidenced great care. Beside her stood a large woman, older, and more the personality type.

McDevin, Crolley, and Canyon stood up politely. "Good evening, ladies," said Mike suavely. "Permit me to introduce myself. I am Lieutenant Michael McDevin, and these are my disreputable companions; Lieutenant Dick Crolley, a navigator of dubious worth, from Springfield, a small village in Ohio. And this is Lieutenant Bill Canyon, our aircraft chauffeur, who lives on an Indian reservation in Iowa."

"He always gets the drop on me," said Crolley. "McDevin's

a toggler, but they call him a bombadier. He hails from an obscure irrigation ditch in Wyoming."

"Well, I am Roberta Palgovitch and this is Mildred Ames," sang the brown-eyed nurse. "I hope you don't mind our sharing your table, but there was a long line out there, and we didn't want to wait, and . . ."

"Okay, Bert, that's enough," interrupted Mildred. "They get the idea. Do we rest the chassis or do we eat standing up?"

"Oh, I beg your pardon," apologized McDevin. "How stupid of me. Won't you please sit down?"

"Shall we pair off, or just sit anywhere?" asked Mildred.

"Pair off, by all means," said Crolley.

"Well, do you choose or do we?" asked Mildred.

"Oh, Mildred," scolded Roberta. "What will the boys think?"

"Just what they've been thinking ever since we got here," said Mildred. "Where do I park the body?"

"How about taking a chance with me?" asked McDevin. "I've always wanted to get gay with a captain."

"Get gay with me, Buster, and you'll get a right cross to the jaw," warned Mildred, meaningfully, and sat down in the chair offered by McDevin.

"Oh, she doesn't mean it really," gushed Roberta. "She just has an inferiority complex. I'm on the psychopathic ward at the hospital and I recognize those things."

"Yeah, and I'm Gunga Din," said Mildred. "She carries bedpans in my ward and the closest thing we got to a mental case is a colonel with the D. T.'s."

Crolley offered Roberta a chair and called the waiter. Canyon, seeing that he was going to be the extra in the crowd, gave McDevin one pound ten to cover his share of the meal and took off. The girls ordered drinks and food, and McDevin and Crolley, coffee.

After they had finished dinner, at the suggestion of Roberta, the four of them went to the girls' room, which was in the hotel.

"I've got a bottle of bourbon," she said, as they got on the elevator. "I thought we could have some cocktails before we go out, since you were so nice to ask us."

"I'm glad it's bourbon," said McDevin. "You know, it's a funny thing, when I was in the States I only drank Scotch occasionally, because Scotch is expensive. But now that I'm over here, and I can't get bourbon, I'm getting tired of Scotch."

"I never get tired of anything with alcohol in it," said Crolley.

"I'm an old booze hound myself," confessed Mildred. "When Twinkle Toes here comes up with this bottle of bourbon the other day I tried to buy it all for myself, but she wanted to keep it and divide it with somebody. I told her we could divide something else with somebody, so here we are drinking what should be mine."

By this time they were out of the elevator and Roberta unlocked the door of their room. True to her word, she drew a bottle of bonded bourbon whiskey from her overnight bag and poured a drink all around.

"Why don't you turn on the radio?" asked Mildred. "Maybe we can hear Lord Haw Haw, or maybe we can even get some music."

"Try to get Armed Forces Radio," suggested Roberta. "They've always got some jive." And she turned off the main light in the room, leaving only a small table lamp burning.

"Now ain't this going to be cozy," said McDevin. "Soft lights, soft music, and beautiful women. All we need is champagne."

"Hell, we got whiskey," said Crolley. "What do you want, blood?"

"No, just champagne," said McDevin, walking over to the phone. He lifted the receiver and waited.

"Room service, beverage, please. Hello, beautiful. Send me up two bottles of chilled champagne. . . . Vintage? Hell, I don't care. Send up something good. What do you have? . . . That sounds good. How much is that? Seven pound ten! Good God, lady, haven't you got anything cheaper? . . . Yeah, that sounds better. . . . Send some up." He hung up the receiver. "See there?" he said. "When you're with McDevin you want for nothing."

"And that's what you get," said Crolley.

Roberta was taking off her shoes and stockings. "I hope you don't mind if I take off some of these clothes. It'll only take me a minute. Besides, I want to change before we go out."

"Hell, you can take them all off, as far as I'm concerned," said Crolley. "But you'd better watch out for McDevin; he doesn't believe in those things."

"Speak for yourself, John," said McDevin. "I can stand as much of it as you can."

Roberta had walked over and sat down by Crolley who was lying on the bed, drink in hand. Crolley slipped an arm around her waist and said, "That was a fatal mistake, baby. Once I get 'em on a bed, they've had it."

"Lieutenant, you scare me to death," giggled Roberta.

"Yeah, just like Jekyll scared Hyde," said Mildred.

"What are you doing away across the room?" said McDevin coyly to Mildred.

"Sittin' on the only thing the Army hasn't taken away from me," she answered severely.

"You don't have to sit way across the room to do that," said McDevin.

"Maybe not," answered Mildred, "but I don't believe in leaving any vulnerable sectors unguarded."

"Is that kind of a left-handed compliment?" asked McDevin. "Do you mean if I made love to you, you couldn't resist me?"

"It's not me I'm afraid for, sonny, it's you."

"Don't let her scare you out, Mike," said Roberta, as she set Crolley's drink on the floor and lay down beside him. "She has an inferiority complex and it takes her awhile to get started."

"Listen, baby," said Crolley. "How about giving all your attention to me. I rape easy."

"So does an orangutan," said Mildred from the corner.

"I wouldn't know," said Roberta. "I haven't dated an orangutan lately."

"Come, come, children," said McDevin. "Flattery will get you nowhere!" And he got up and walked over to Mildred. "Well, if you won't sit in my lap," he said, "let's dance. No use wasting that beautiful music."

"I know it's just a sly trick to wear down my resistance, but let me give you a clue, Jackson," warned Mildred. "Lay one hand on me and you'll regret it." As she spoke there was a knock at the door.

"Oh, hell," cursed Crolley. "Interruptions, always interruptions."

"Must be the champagne," forecast McDevin as he opened the door.

McDevin's prediction was correct; the champagne had arrived. But the hotel manager had arrived with it. He was a wizened character with horn-rimmed glasses and a cutaway coat. He was very thin and his skin was tightly drawn over protruding bones. A high forehead swept away from a long pointed nose and his lips were small and pinched together. He carried a handkerchief in the left sleeve of his coat and his attitude was one of arrogance and self-righteousness. His voice was strained and high-pitched.

"I say," he began briskly. "This *is* a bit thick. After all, we're not running a common house, you know. This is one of London's most respected hostelries, and we're not accustomed to compromising situations. What I mean is, you simply can't do this."

"Why not?" asked Crolley simply.

"It isn't done," he said with a touch of irritation.

"What isn't done?" asked McDevin.

"Please, don't be difficult. You know very well what I mean. A congregation of two sexes of even numbers in a hotel room usually means only one thing. You must leave here at once."

"We weren't doing anything," protested Roberta. "We were just listening to the radio and having a few drinks. There's no law against that, even in Britain."

"Never mind," the manager said shortly. "I've been in the hotel business for twenty-two years and I fancy myself quite a judge."

"Well unfancy yourself and limp off, Dan," said Crolley with derision.

"If you don't leave immediately, I shall summon a bobby, and mark my words, you'll be dealt with severely. Now come, come, get along with you."

"Well, wait until I put my shoes on," whined Roberta.

"I should have known you were in a state of half dress," said the manager. "But never mind, I mean only for the gentlemen to leave. You ladies must stay here."

"What do you mean we must stay here?" demanded Mildred.

"I won't allow you to leave until the gentlemen are out of the hotel. I knew when I saw you board the elevator that I should have stopped you then. But I must insist the gentlemen leave the hotel completely before you ladies leave the room. I shall notify you by 'phone when they are safely gone."

"You're a high-handed sort of a jerk," said Mildred, piqued. "I paid for these rooms and I'll come and go when I damn please."

"Please," said the manager. "You should consider yourself fortunate that I haven't asked you to give up the rooms entirely.

I assure you that if you weren't ladies, or rather, since you are not men, I shouldn't hesitate a moment to throw you bodily from the hotel. But I realize that it would be next to impossible for you to find lodging elsewhere this time of the evening."

"Now listen here . . ." began Mildred.

"Tut, tut," admonished the manager. "After all, you are officers and I assume that you are ladies. I do not consider you of the same ilk as the promiscuous females who clutter the doorway of my hotel. Now, I have given you the benefit of the doubt. I have not inquired as to your activities immediately previous to my appearance in your room. I believe that I have been more than genial. If you gentlemen will gather together your belongings and depart the hotel quickly, I, and my entire staff, shall be most grateful to you. I'll give you five minutes. At the end of that time if you are not away, I shall call the authorities." And he turned on his heel and started to leave. But he stopped suddenly. "The champagne was five pounds."

"I'll get it," said Mildred. "No use for you guys to pay for it if you don't get to drink any of it."

"How about meeting us some place later?" asked Crolley.

"Oh, I think that's a wonderful idea," said Roberta.

"No, I've shot my wad for the night," said Mildred. "Besides, we've got to catch an early morning train."

"But Mildred . . ." protested Roberta.

"Never mind, Godiva, there's plenty of men back at the hospital."

"Oh, all right," answered Roberta, dejectedly.

"Well, how about me?" said Crolley. "I won't be there."

"You'll live, Buster," said Mildred. "There's plenty of women at the door of the hotel. Get him out of here, Mike, before we all get in trouble."

"Okay," answered McDevin. "I'll see you around. Want to kiss me good-night?"

"That's futile," answered Mildred. "Just get the hell out of here before we get in trouble. After all, that pipsqueak could call a cop and if the Old Man ever got word of this, our goose would be cooked."

"Well, hell, we weren't doing anything," protested McDevin. "They couldn't have proved a thing."

"Look, woodenhead, let me draw you a picture. Everybody

from the hospital commander down to the latrine orderly knows that Roberta suffers from nymphomania. Get it? Hot pants. And the Old Man would take it for granted. Now, would you please leave? I didn't come along on this little jaunt to have a good time. I came along to keep Roberta out of trouble, and as far as I'm concerned, she's gone too far already."

"Okay," said McDevin. "I can take a hint."

Crolley and Roberta had retired to a dark corner of the room and were oblivious of Mildred's and Mike's conversation. After a considerable harangue on the part of McDevin, he finally convinced Crolley, with a promise of greener fields, to leave. They left the hotel through the front door and were accosted immediately by another raft of Piccadilly commandos. They pushed their way through the crowd, following one of the streets that fanned from the circus. They passed a newsreel movie theater half a block down. McDevin suggested they go in, but he was over-ruled strenuously by Crolley, who argued that such a move would be a waste of valuable time, and they walked onward. Cockney newsboys, fifty and over, hawked papers on the curb: "Pyper, pyper," they shouted, loud and clear.

"Why don't you buy a paper, Mike?" suggested Crolley. "We can read it before we go to bed."

"That's just a cover-up, you damn fool," said McDevin. "You know what they're selling just as well as I do."

"What time is it?" asked Crolley.

"Twenty minutes to ten," answered McDevin. "What difference does it make? We got all night."

"But we haven't made any progress yet," objected Crolley. "If it hadn't been for that little sawed-off manager and that draft mare named Mildred, about now would be my time to crow," and he gave a silly giggle.

"Yeah, I know," answered McDevin, registering distaste. "If you want laughs, just look around you. Look at all these old whores runnin' after this American money. It's a damn rotten shame. You know it, Crolley."

"Yeah, disgraceful," mocked Crolley.

"We shouldn't be here ourselves, you know that, Dick? Here we are in a city of eight million people, the heart of the world's greatest empire, right in the very guts of the most colorful town in the world, and we're dodgin' prostitutes and phony newsboys. It makes me sick to think about it."

"Well, careful where you aim it," muttered Crolley.

"You know, Dick," mused McDevin. "Someday I'm going to write a book about all this."

"Yeah? What are you going to call it?"

" 'A Yank on Piccadilly.' Yeah, and it's going to be about you and me, Dick, from the time we hit Liverpool until we leave for home."

"What makes you think we'll live through it? I don't like this combat worth a damn."

"Well, if we don't live through it, tough. They'll have to find somebody else to write the Great American Novel."

"Jeezis, Mike, we're not gettin' anywhere just walkin'."

"Well, when did you tell Roberta you'd meet her?"

"How did you know about that?" asked Crolley, surprised.

"Listen, you little knucklehead. I been eatin', sleepin', flyin', and everything else with you for over six months now, and I know you pretty well. Besides, if I'd been in your shoes, I would have done the same thing."

"Well, I told her I'd meet her in the Court Club."

"The Court Club? Where in the hell is that?"

"Don't you remember?" asked Dick. "Old Hal Barton gave us the lowdown on the Court Club after our first mssion. He said it was good for drinkin' and there's always lots of women there. They've got a piano there, too. I thought you might sing four or five hundred dirty songs. That always lures the quiff around, you know, and you can kinda take your pick. When they bend over a piano you can kinda walk around behind and check the hips. That's always a good gauge to use, big hips, big heart; little hips, cold as a dog's nose."

"Where did you get that rule of thumb?" asked McDevin.

"My old man fingered it out. Did you get that, Mike?"

"Yeah, I know," sighed McDevin. "Joe Miller again."

"Let's get to the Court Club now," urged Crolley. "Maybe we can line up a quail for you before Roberta gets there, and one for me in case she can't get away from old dragon puss."

"Okay," said McDevin. "Get out and lie down in the street and maybe a cab will stop."

"It's cheaper to go by tube," said Crolley. "The Court Club is only about four blocks from the Cumberland Hotel. We can go back to the Piccadilly station and take the subway to Marble Arch and walk down."

"Hell with that noise," said McDevin. "I'm not going to fight that crowd again," and he hailed the next cab.

The Court Club was a den of iniquity, literally, and was located just off Oxford Street, a few blocks down from the Cumberland Hotel. Its proprietor was a short, red-faced, happy-go-lucky little chap named Maury, and it was a typical London bottle club, supported by American soldiers, and frequented by a host of indiscriminate women judiciously provided by Maury to supply the American patrons with lecherous companionship. These girls were called "hostesses" and were for the most part women who preferred the relatively easy life of prostitution, or semi-prostitution, to that of work in the British war plants. Like the Piccadilly commandos, they were young, and in many cases very attractive. They hung around the club from late afternoon, when it opened, until eleven o'clock at night, when it closed. During this time they gave their complete attention to the various American patrons who came in for a drink or to get drunk, and urged them to buy additional drinks for both themselves and the hostesses. During the latter part of an evening, they would latch on to some of the more prosperous customers and indicate, ever so slightly, their willingness to spend the night with them. When the Court Club closed, they would take their catches to another bottle club, run either by Maury or somebody else of dubious integrity. There they would remain until two or three o'clock in the morning, when they would take their quarry home or to his hotel room.

In order to enter the Court Club, or any of its counterparts, one had to be a "member." The initial cost of membership was ten shillings, the equivalent at that time of about two dollars in American money. One was provided with an identification card and from then on, by flashing this card and paying ten shillings on each occasion, one was allowed to enter the club and partake of its beverage at five shillings per highball.

These clubs were permitted to stay open only for a period of five or six hours. Some clubs chose from six to eleven. Others took care of the suckers from eleven until three.

The proprietors became rich, using as a guide the basic theory that an American wanted liquor and sex at any price. They would even sell a fifth of Scotch for the small monetary remuneration of four pounds, ten shillings, or the then equivalent of eighteen dollars, thirteen and a half cents. They were happy to have their customers drink it in the clubs and would sell splash, their counterpart of American soda, and a bowl of ice for five shilling per setup. If a patron liked company, they provided girls to help him drink his eighteen-dollar whiskey. And when there were not enough girls to go around, the waiters and musicians would wander about, bumming a drink wherever they could. They took their drinks straight, and instead of drinking them with you, they carried their whiskey to a back room where they poured it into a bottle. By the time the club closed, each had a fifth of whiskey of his own— all free of charge.

The entrepreneur missed no chance to squeeze as much as he could from every sucker who entered his establishment. Provided a guest's billet was within a radius of one mile of his club, he would furnish transportation for only thirteen shillings a head. As a matter of fact, his cars, run illegally on black-market petrol, stood by all evening for the convenience of his customers—if they could pay, of course. But despite the price that he had to pay, and pay, and pay, the American—the world's greatest sucker— loved it.

McDevin and Crolley entered the front door of the Court Club and were met by a cheerful blonde with a big smile and outstretched palm. She checked their hats for two shillings sixpence apiece. With an attitude of extreme confidence, not bothering to ask their desires in the matter, having solicited literally hundreds of American memberships, she asked them a few routine questions, required them to sign their names, and, for ten shillings apiece, she allowed them to enter the club. It was a room about thirty feet wide and sixty feet long with a twenty-foot bar on the far longitudinal wall. There were numerous stools around the bar and comfortable chairs along each side of the room. At the rear was a piano and an address system, close to a small dance floor about ten feet square. Two stools at the bar were empty, and McDevin and Crolley moved to them quickly for the place was very crowded. A well-dressed barmaid took their orders and served them promptly.

"There you are, gentlemen," she said brightly. "Two Scotch. That'll be ten shillings, please."

"Ten shillings!" exclaimed Crolley. "Does the gun go with it?"

"I beg your pardon?" she asked.

"Forget it," he said. "Here's your blood money."

"We haven't much time," said McDevin. "Do you see Roberta?"

"No, but she thought she might be late. She said she would have to slip away from old cantankerous. It's five minutes past ten now. If she's not here in half an hour, I'll start huntin' for other quail."

"Well, you won't have to hunt far," answered McDevin. "Just look around you. I'll lay you odds that if we buy enough drinks we'll be approached by some of these babes for an all night stand. Just look at them."

"Some aren't bad," said Crolley, leering at a redhead across the room.

"Let me give you fair warning now, Dick," said McDevin. "It's not worth it. These women are the lowest form of life, and you're a damn fool if you let them take you in."

"Oh, I don't know," said Crolley. "Maybe you'll find a clean one."

"I wouldn't count on it," said McDevin. "I get kind of a kick out of watching them, though, don't you?"

"You'll get a whole lot more than that," answered Crolley, "when they come over here and ask you to buy them a drink. There's no one playing that piano back there, Mike. Why don't you go back and knock off a few ditties and liven the joint up?"

"I don't know," said McDevin dubiously. "Maybe the proprietor wouldn't like it."

"How do you know unless you try?" challenged Crolley. "The thing is just sittin' back there ready to be played, and apparently they don't have a regular entertainer."

"How do you know?" asked McDevin.

"Well, you don't see a kitty out there, do you? I haven't seen an Englishman yet that didn't have his hand out."

"That doesn't mean anything," protested McDevin. "When you come right down to it, with very few exceptions, we've seen only the lower class of people. If I were you, I wouldn't discount the limeys a damn bit. And don't judge them by those you see in the bars. I'll wager that if we sought the same element at home that we have since we've been here in London, you could bet your

107

bottom peso that the only way you could tell the difference would be by the accent."

"Oh, for crying out loud, Mike," complained Crolley. "Don't wax philosophical on me now. Why don't you just shut up and go back and play the piano?"

"Okay," said McDevin. "I'll go struggle with the keys, but if they throw me out, I'm going to see to it that they throw you out right along with me."

McDevin and Crolley walked nonchalantly back to the piano, carefully eyeing each female as they went.

"What do they do to you in England for mental rape?" mused Crolley.

Mike tested the piano with a few well-chosen chords and found that it was surprisingly well tuned and had excellent action. It was a small upright, but even its pianissimo was moderately loud.

Immediately, several couples made their way to the piano and some went to the dance floor, assuming that McDevin could produce danceable music. He began his program easily with *I'm Getting Sentimental Over You* and then, with a knowing look at Crolley, he played *Black Magic*. No one made an attempt to throw him out. The applause was kind so he pushed on to greater and better things. His next rendition was a song he had learned over a bottle of Scotch at the Officers' Club one night with a guy named Dave Reed, entitled *I Want to Play with Your Poodle*. It was jumpy little number with a dissonance-dominated, bluesy accompaniment, and racy lyrics that went something like this:

> *I want to play with your poodle,*
> *I want to play with your poodle,*
> *I want to play with your poodle,*
> *I mean your little poodle dog.*
> *It's cool in the summer,*
> *It's warm in the fall,*
> *I like your poodle 'cause it's so small.*
> *I want to play with your poodle,*
> *I mean your little poodle dog.*

With the added attraction of spice, the crowd around the piano began to grow. *Star Dust* and *Rhapsody in Blue* gave way by popular demand to *Roll Me Over in the Clover, Roll Me Over,*

Lay Me Down and Do It Again and McDevin's own naughty parody on *Five Foot Two*. By this time the more generous members in the crowd, who were being "sent" by McDevin's musical manifestations, had begun to supply Mike with far more Scotch than he could drink, or deserved.

He played *The Eyes of Texas* four times at the insistence of a huge, belligerent captain from San Antonio who called his buddy "a damned Yankee from Dallas—North Texas, that is." In the middle of a very disgraceful take-off of a very decent and beautiful song Roberta entered, gay and inviting. She made her way straight to Crolley and kissed him soundly. Her eyes were shining and her beautiful, flushed face, framed by radiant hair, set off her full lips. For safety's sake, Crolley escorted her to the dance floor and began methodical, unrhythmical gyrations. He held Roberta close and she slipped quietly into a world all her own, far removed from this earth of ours, high in the clouds. She anticipated what she considered to be the acme of ecstasies, and she was enjoying herself immensely. Crolley's animal instinct was beginning to show, and McDevin's fingers, oiled by excessive quantities of Scotch, were creating such unusual and pleasing chord combinations, and arranging them in such effective sequences, that nearly everyone in the room was emotionally aroused. Only a few times in his hit-and-miss musical career had McDevin ever produced music commensurate with his capabilities. This was one of those times. He remembered all the tunes that he thought he had forgotten, played many that he had never heard before, and "took-off" on choruses that would have been the envy of even the great Duke Ellington. He had reached a point of excellence never before attained, he thought—and such an appreciative audience.

While he was doing his own jazz version of *Onward Christian Soldiers,* giving emphasis on unusual chord structure and bright cadenzas, he felt light hands on his shoulders. Upon observation, he found the fingers to be well manicured, of exceptional beauty, and strangely familiar. When his number was over and the applause had subsided, and amidst demanding calls for encore, he heard a low, rich voice from behind him say, "You owe me ten shillings, Mike, for my fare into this terrible place."

He turned around quickly in surprise and exclaimed, "Linda!"

109

8

M c DEVIN STOOD UP SUDDENLY.

"What are you doing here?" he exclaimed in utter surprise.

"I came to see you, Mike," she replied softly. She looked lovingly into his face and continued, "I'm sorry, Mike, honestly I am. I'm making a complete fool of myself, I know. But I had to see you."

"Your timing was perfect. How did you know where to find me?"

"When you and Dick were in Cambridge you talked many times about the Court Club, and when they told me at your base that you were on pass, well . . . here I am."

"I thought you couldn't get away from work," stated McDevin.

"My supervisor gave me a holiday. I have two whole days to be with you," and then she added gently, lowering her eyes, "if you want me."

"Want you! Of course, I want you! Where are you staying?"

"I arrived on a late train and I came here straightway. I was afraid I'd miss you."

"I don't know where we are going to get you a room. It's past eleven already, and I haven't the faintest idea where to look," he said in despair.

Linda shrugged her shoulders.

"Look," said Mike. "Let me buy us a drink and we'll get Crolley and talk the situation over."

Mike's audience meanwhile was protesting his absence from the keyboard, but when he ignored their urgings to return, they began to drift away. Crolley and Roberta had taken a seat across the room from the piano and were completely engrossed in each other. McDevin took Linda to the bar and ordered two Scotch and sodas.

"I've made a mess of things, as usual," said Linda sadly. "Please don't think too badly of me."

"I'm damned glad you came. Now I'll have someone to do the town with. First, we'll catch a cab and try all the hotels. As soon as we find you a place to stay, we'll take in some all-night bottle clubs and have a good time."

They took their drinks toward the back of the club and sat down next to Dick and Roberta.

"Hey, knucklehead, come up for air before you smother. Look who's here."

Crolley was startled. When he saw Linda, he exclaimed, "What the hell are you doing here, Linda? Did you bring Doris?" He stopped suddenly, catching himself, then continued, "That *is* your mother's name, isn't it? Doris?" Without waiting for her reply, he said, "Linda, may I introduce Roberta? Roberta, this is Linda, McDevin's United Kingdom sweetheart. She's from Cambridge. Roberta's a nurse, as you can see, Linda." The girls looked each other over.

"Delighted," said Linda coolly.

"Likewise," replied Roberta.

"Now wait a minute," said McDevin. "Let's chip off some of the ice. We've all got to be friends if we expect to have a good time. Roberta is Crolley's girl and Linda is my girl. I'm not going to get fresh with Roberta and Crolley won't get fresh with Linda —I don't think. Everybody agree?"

"What'll we do now?" asked Crolley. "This joint is about to close. Maury is up front with his bowels in an uproar 'cause we're still here and he's ready to lock up."

They all started toward the door. Crolley picked up their wraps and they joined the crowd waiting for taxis.

"The first thing we've got to do," said McDevin, "is find a room for Linda. Anybody got any suggestions?"

"It's too late for that now," said Roberta. "I don't know where you could get a room in London at this time of night."

"You made a mistake, Mike," announced Crolley. "I got news for you. Our problem, Mr. Anthony, is not to find Linda a room, but to find you and Linda *both* a room. Roberta has just consented to be my paramour—for tonight, anyhow."

"You *are* abrupt!" exclaimed Linda.

"Maybe so," said Crolley, "but that's how the wind blows."

"Now wait a minute," protested McDevin. "Where do you get off? I'm not about to give up my sack. If you and Roberta want to sleep together, go find your own room. It'll be a cold day in hell when I give up my bed."

111

"Let me refresh your memory," said Crolley. "It seems to me that I recall a night about five months ago when we were stationed at Ardmore and we took a little trip down to Dallas. You locked me out of our little boudoir in the Baker Hotel and I wandered the streets for the rest of the night. I got picked up by the cops for loitering, while you laid up there all night with some beautiful babe."

"I wasn't with a beautiful babe," denied McDevin. "I locked the door from the inside and passed out. I didn't hear you knock."

"That's your story."

"This isn't getting me a room," protested Linda. "Besides I'm not at all up to listening to stories of what appears to be a very sordid past."

"Get *her*," said Roberta, under her breath.

"I got it!" cried Dick.

"So you admit it," cracked McDevin. "Wait till Doc Lerdner hears about this."

"Aw, blow it! I'm just trying to help you. Here I solve your problems and you make snide remarks."

"Quit acting like children," said Linda. "What's the solution?"

"Well, it's only about eleven-thirty. Canyon hasn't been in bed over three hours. Let's go get him up and send him over to the Red Cross Officers' Club and then you can have our room and we'll take his."

"If I were Canyon, I shouldn't like that," said Linda.

"Who says he'll like it," answered Crolley. "He'll bitch like hell, but he'll do it."

"I don't know," said McDevin dubiously. "He doesn't approve .of our antics. And the way he likes to sleep, I think he would take a dim view of being rousted out in the middle of the night."

"Let him," argued Crolley. "He'll get over it in a day or two. What right has he got to waste a bed by sleeping in it?"

"Aren't you being a bit presumptuous?" protested Linda. "You said Mike and I would share a room. I value my chastity much too much for that sort of thing."

"I am Jesus' little lamb, I'm a good girl, yes I am," murmured Roberta sardonically.

"Well, let's try it. At least, you will have a place to sleep," said Mike quickly. "We can walk to the hotel; it's only four blocks away." And he began to move away rapidly, pulling Linda with him.

"I don't like that girl," said Linda.

"Not so loud," warned McDevin. "They're right behind us."

In five minutes they were at the door of the Cumberland. They stopped just outside.

"How'll we work this?" asked McDevin. "We can't just walk in. They'll know something is fishy."

"Maybe they like fish," said Crolley.

"Be serious, you dope," admonished McDevin. "If we all four walk up together, they're bound to suspect us and throw us out."

"You're right," agreed Linda. "They will that. I have a suggestion. Let Roberta and me go in together, and in ten minutes you two come in. She has her uniform on and they surely wouldn't suspect her of immoral conduct."

"You sing pretty," said Roberta, "but you have the lyrics wrong."

"None the less, let's give it a try. What room is it?"

"801," answered Mike. "But we don't have the key."

"There's where you're wrong," said Crolley, coming to the rescue. "I learned but when a wee lad, never to go without my hotel key. It's so handy for emergencies." He handed Roberta the key and she and Linda went inside.

McDevin and Crolley leaned up against the building and lighted cigarettes.

"Bill's not going to like this, Dick, and I don't blame him a damn bit."

"Well, like I said before," answered Crolley, "he'll bitch to high heaven, but when we tell him this is an emergency, I'm sure he'll agree."

"But where in the hell is he going to get a room?"

"In the Red Cross Club, like I said."

"I know, I know, but which one? There must be a thousand of them here. How do you know they'll have any vacant sacks? Hell, I think there are more Americans in London than Englishmen."

"Listen," said Crolley. "Do you think the Red Cross is going to let a man down in time of disaster? They'll have a sack *some* place for him. Besides, Bill sleeps too much, anyhow. It'd do him good to stay up all night. Maybe he'd use up some of that energy

113

that helps him beat that goddamn coal pail and sing *Old Black Magic*."

"You know, Dick, when you get on the trail of a hot dame, you lose all sense of reason."

"That's why I get more than most men."

"If I were single I'd run you a close race."

"If you were single, my foot. Don't give me that song and dance," snickered Crolley. "By the way, Mike, somethin's been botherin' me all night."

"What's the matter?"

"It's Linda's showing up here. Funny how she knew where we were, and when we were on pass. They don't give out that kind of information at the base."

"Yeah, I've been thinking the same thing myself."

"And another thing. Have you noticed how she's been yapping right at the proper time about her chastity? And she called me presumptuous because I suggested you and she share our room. But you notice she's falling right along with the plan. She hasn't tried to back out, and it was her idea how to get past the room clerk and house dick."

"Well, I've never had any illusions about Linda. She's no virgin—and hasn't been for years, I'll bet. I just don't think she's as free and easy as girls like Doris or Roberta."

"Maybe you're right, but if I were you, I'd watch my step. For my money, she's a slick operator. Besides that, she keeps giving you that 'sick calf' look all the time. If I were you, I'd lay her and leave her."

"No dice. I told you how I felt."

Crolley flipped his cigarette to the street and said with a sigh, "Listen, buddy, this is Crolley. You know as well as I do, if you sleep in the same room with her tonight, you're going to wind up making love. I don't care who you are. If you don't mind my saying so, your actions aren't compatible with your thinking. Of course, I'm just judging from how you talk. But if you were so dead set against stepping out on your wife, you wouldn't have a damn thing to do with her. If you actually believe the way you talk, you would have taken in a movie tonight and hit the sack about ten o'clock, instead of gettin' half polluted and putting yourself in a position where some gal serves it to you on a silver platter. Course, it's your own business, but if you want to remain true to Katherine, let Linda have your room and you go to the Red Cross Club. Or else sleep with Canyon, and Roberta and I will take our room."

"Canyon snores," commented McDevin simply. "Let's go upstairs."

Moments later, Crolley and McDevin knocked on the door of 801.

Roberta opened the door an inch and peered out cautiously. "I thought you were the manager," she said with relief. "The room clerk gave us a cold fishy stare when we came up. I think he was suspicious."

"Well, he hasn't any idea where you went, so even if he were suspicious he probably couldn't find you," said Crolley.

"We played it smart," said Roberta. "We took the elevator to the tenth floor, then walked back down here to the eighth. That will throw the elevator operator off. It was Linda's idea."

"Well, for Christ sake, close the door," exclaimed McDevin. "We'll awaken everybody on the floor with our yapping and they'll know where you are for sure."

Roberta obeyed with one last look into the hall, to make absolutely sure no one was there.

Linda was stretched out comfortably on the big double bed. She was smoking a cigarette and there was a look of complete relaxation on her face. She lay with her free arm above her head and her trim ankles crossed. Her dress was just above her knees. Roberta had removed her shoes and stockings, taken off her blouse, removed her tie and unbuttoned her shirt, exposing a brassière and bare midriff.

"You look inviting, stretched out there, Linda," said McDevin.

"I feel inviting, too," she said.

"Well, let's hurry up and get started," said Roberta. "The night's half gone." Then, conscious of her obvious impatience, she added hastily, "I mean if this is going to be a party, let's have a drink and turn on the radio."

"Quick recovery," commented Linda.

"Why don't you dig out the bottle, Dick?" suggested McDevin. "I could use a short one."

"Why don't you take your short one over in Canyon's room?" responded Crolley.

"Aw, come on, Dick," said McDevin. "It's only midnight. You

115

got until nine o'clock tomorrow morning before the maids come in. Fifteen or twenty minutes is not going to hurt you any."

"Oh, Mike," protested Linda. "Must we always keep our conversation on such a low plane? I don't believe I've ever heard you and Dick talk about anything else. Really, it's beginning to wear on my nerves."

"Oh, brother," said Roberta softly.

"Maybe you're right," said McDevin. "Perhaps we should talk about something else. But before we talk about anything, I can offer you whiskey two ways, straight or with water."

"Who cares?" said Crolley impatiently. "Just pour 'em."

McDevin procured four water glasses from the bathroom, poured each of them half full, and passed them around.

"Really, Mike, I can't drink that much."

"Oh, go ahead," urged Mike. "It'll put hair on your chest."

Linda laughed. "I'm a bit tired," she said. "Maybe it will perk me up." She sat up on the edge of the bed, offered her glass in toast, and said, "Cheers." Everyone followed suit. Crolley, who was eager to get Linda and Mike out of the room, gulped his whiskey and consumed nearly half of it in the first drink. Roberta drank the entire contents of her glass. McDevin took Linda to the large chair and pulled her down on his lap. They sipped their drinks casually.

"Don't you think it's time to go send Canyon out of there?" said Crolley.

"Take it easy and turn on the radio," said McDevin.

"There's nothing on after twelve o'clock," said Crolley. "What the hell you waiting on, old home week? You can do everything you're doing here over there."

"We love your company," teased Linda.

Crolley made no reply. Roberta had lain down on the bed with her head against the backboard. She held her second drink in one hand, cigarette in the other, and whimsically regarded her carefully painted toes, as she wiggled them rhythmically.

Linda and Mike had struck up a conversation about Cambridge University. Dick sat dejectedly on the floor by the dresser and drank straight shots. He had taken the bottle with him to avoid getting up and down.

Without looking up, Roberta said, "By rights, I should go back and see how Mildred is getting along. There's nothing doing here," and she looked at Crolley meaningly.

Crolley took the hint and said quickly, "The hell with dragon puss. She can get along all right by herself." Then he turned belligerently to McDevin. "Now, goddam it, Mike, you've never acted like this before, since I've known you. Go over and get Canyon out of bed and leave Roberta and me alone, will you? It's a quarter past twelve already."

Linda got up from his lap, and taking both glasses she poured another drink.

"But I don't think Linda and I ought to go over there together. After all, Bill will be in bed, and you know how he is when he first wakes up. Besides he can't dress in front of Linda."

"She's seen naked men before," muttered Roberta. Linda whirled around.

"I've had about enough of you and your nasty remarks. Apparently American women are as crude as American men. One more insinuation like that from you and I'll snatch out your bloody hair."

"*Tsk, tsk,* mama's litle girl had better watch out or she'll end up with a fat lip," said Roberta, still regarding her toes.

Linda was breathing heavily.

"Why don't you two call a truce?" suggested McDevin. "Fighting isn't going to get us anywhere."

"Yeah, lay off, Roberta," said Crolley.

"I'm sorry," apologized Linda. "I realize that I irritate you. I shan't lose my temper again, but I do wish you would try to be more civil toward me."

"Let's go try to wake Bill up, Mike. You girls wait here—try to keep from slitting each other's throat."

McDevin and Crolley went quietly out into the hall, walked around the corner of the corridor, and knocked softly on Canyon's door. There was no answer. They knocked several times, but no one stirred inside.

"We'll never wake that guy up this way," lamented Crolley. "Let's go back to the room and call him."

"If we do that," answered McDevin, "he'll never let us in the room. We've got to get in some way."

"Maybe our key will fit," suggested Crolley. "Wait a minute. I'll go back and get it."

"I'll be damned if I'll stand out here in the hall and wait for you," said McDevin.

The two hurried back to number 801.

"Back so soon?" said Linda.

"Uh-huh," said Crolley. "We can't wake him. We thought we'd try our key in his door."

"It won't fit," said Linda with decision. "The hotel wouldn't dare install locks with interchangeable keys, especially on the same floor. You'll need a pass key."

"But where are we going to get it?" asked McDevin.

"This is a hell of a note," cried Crolley in annoyance. "Everything happens to me. I knew it was too good to be true."

Roberta sat up abruptly. She asked, "How many keys do you have to this room?"

"Just one," answered Crolley.

"Well, whose key is that behind the water pitcher on the dresser? It's under the towel. I saw it when I was nosing around while we were waiting for you two."

Crolley was over by the dresser like a shot. He lifted the towel and picked up the key. "It's to Canyon's room!" he almost shouted. "Oh, happy day, he must have left it here this evening. I remember laying this towel down after I shaved."

"This is all very convenient," said Linda. "It's almost like a story."

"Well, let's go! Let's go!" said Crolley with excitement.

"I wonder how Canyon got into his room?" pondered McDevin. "Maybe he's not in yet."

"He probably got the extra key from the desk," said Crolley. "Who cares? The important thing is, we've got the key."

"But if he's not in," said McDevin, "he'll be mighty surprised to find his room occupied when he does come back."

"That's your worry," said Crolley. "Come on, let's get the hell out of here."

"Wait a minute," said McDevin. "If he hasn't got his key, he'll get another one from the desk, and then he'll walk right in on us. I don't mind so much, but it will be mighty embarrassing to Linda."

"We won't be in bed, anyhow," said Linda. "At least, not together."

"Hah," whooped Roberta. She had reached to the depths of

118

her diaphragm and forced up the expletive with great violence, and it cascaded out of her mouth like water out of a fireplug, leaving no doubt as to its innuendo.

"I warned you," said Linda coldly.

"Wait a minute, girls, wait a minute," said Crolley. "This is neither the time nor the place. We've got this damn thing solved now. Let's not ruin it."

McDevin sat down suddenly on the bed. Then he casually stretched out, reached for a cigarette, and a smug look spread over his face. "I just happened to recall," he said, "that when you suggested the whole thing, Dick, you said you and Roberta would take Canyon's room and let Linda and me have this one."

Crolley was visibly nonplussed. "No, I didn't," he protested weakly.

"I distinctly remember that you did," interposed Linda. "It was just outside the Court Club."

"I'm not going to move," said McDevin, "until you agree."

"Oh, for God's sake," said Roberta, visibly nettled. "I'm going to be an old woman before you get anything done. Let's go to the other room, Dick, and let them have this one. I'm getting damned tired of this. I don't care if Canyon does walk in on us in bed. I'm not a damned bit ashamed of it, if you're not." She began to put her shoes on bare feet.

"Okay," agreed Crolley reluctantly. "But damn you, Mike. I'm going to push you out of a flak hole the first chance I get. Come on, let's go."

McDevin smiled and got up. He drew leisurely on his cigarette and, without hurrying, mashed it out in an ash tray on the dresser. "I'll be right back, girls," he announced.

Crolley was already out in the corridor and within thirty seconds they were at the door of Canyon's room. Crolley stealthily inserted the key in the lock and quietly pushed the door open.

"I wish we had a coal pail," said Crolley, and he reached for the switch and turned on the light which flooded the room.

There was a sudden shriek of female origin, the kind you hear in the movies when the male comedian inadvertently enters a women's restroom. A nude female figure, flashed from a supine position on the bed to a position of rigid attention on the floor. Concurrently with this, there was a spasmodic shout of male origin.

"Goddamn it, what in hell's going on?" came an anguished wail from Bill Canyon.

Within a fraction of a second, he had jumped to his feet in great embarrassment, standing like a lost soul beside Mildred.

There was hysterical laughter on the part of McDevin and Crolley. Canyon and Mildred continued to stand in the same position, somewhat at a loss as to what to say. Canyon began to stutter incoherently and then suddenly burst out in spiteful rage as Mildred hastily crawled back into bed and covered up her head.

"You dirty sons-of-bitches, what's the idea of breakin' in without knockin'?"

"We did knock a minute ago. Why didn't you answer then?" asked Mike.

"Why in the hell do you think I didn't?" answered Canyon contemptuously. "Now get out of here before I cut you both up with a rusty knife."

"Mildred," said Crolley coaxingly. "Show your head or I'll huff and I'll puff until I blow your house in."

Mildred slowly withdrew the sheet from her head. "All right," she said, "you've had your fun, now get the hell out of here."

"If we had only known," said McDevin tauntingly, "we would have made things easier for you."

"Humph," said Mildred, registering doubt. "Where's Roberta?"

"Over in our room," answered Crolley.

"Once you latch onto her," warned Mildred, "you won't be any good for a month."

"How do you know?" asked McDevin.

"I've seen her in action," answered Mildred. "She was born passionate and she's been developing ever since."

"Okay, guys, fun's over. Get out of here," ordered Canyon.

"No, it's just beginning," said Crolley. "Where's your bottle?"

"You know I don't have a bottle," answered Canyon.

"Doc Lerdner gave you one, too," said McDevin. "Anyhow, that's what Porky Terrian told me before we left the base."

"Why do you want to be so holier-than-thou, Bill?" asked Crolley. "Why don't you come right out in the open? What do you think you're gaining by hiding it from Mike and me? It would be a whole lot easier on you and you know damn well we won't tell your wife."

"You told me you weren't married," said Mildred in surprise.

120

"Oh, he's not," said Crolley, quickly realizing his faux pas. "I'm just givin' him a hard time."

"In a pig's eye, you were," said Mildred. "Oh, well, I should worry. I was married once myself. Why did you lie to me, Bill? I would have slept with you, anyhow."

"I'll get even with you guys if it is the last thing I do," threatened Canyon vehemently.

"Aw, grow up," said McDevin. "It's all in fun. You can sleep with every woman in London as far as we're concerned. Why take it so goddamn seriously? Let's go, Dick."

"Go, hell," answered Crolley. "What're we going to do for an extra room?"

"That's your problem," answered McDevin with a laugh.

"The hell it is," said Dick. "Aw, come on, this is your buddy. You wouldn't put Roberta and me outside, would you? Besides, we won't leave, anyhow. You and Linda can sit in a chair."

"Linda?" exclaimed Canyon. "How did that old bitch get here?"

"She's not a bitch," protested McDevin, turning red.

"She must be if she's with you," said Mildred triumphantly.

"Three hours ago you were with me," said McDevin slyly.

"I walked into that one," admitted Mildred.

"Here's our problem," said Crolley. "There's four of us and we've got one room. Anybody got any suggestions?"

"Yeah," muttered Canyon. "Go to hell."

"Why don't we use your room over in the Regent Palace?" suggested McDevin.

"What room?" answered Mildred. "They threw us out of it. Bill and I tried there first. Give a look in the corner," and she pointed across the room. "That's Roberta's and my luggage. And besides that, that little bastard of a manager threatened to notify Eisenhower."

"I wouldn't put it past him," said Crolley. "But what about *our* dilemma? What are we going to do about a place to sleep?"

"I don't care if you never sleep," declared Canyon. "I don't care if I never see you again. I wish you'd drop dead. Is that plain enough? Now get the hell out of here."

"Bill, you surprise me," said Crolley, in mock seriousness. "We didn't know you were so selfish. We thought you'd let us have your room. The way you howled when we came in here, we thought you were ruined for good." Crolley laughed.

"I think we had better go," said McDevin to Dick. "We're just wastin' time. I wouldn't be a bit surprised if Roberta hadn't gone to find herself another man. Any man."

"She's done it before," said Mildred.

There was a slight worry in Crolley's eyes. "Come on, Mike," he said.

"Don't think it ain't been charmin'," said McDevin.

" 'Cause it ain't," amended Canyon, as McDevin slammed the door.

In a matter of seconds Crolley and McDevin were back in 801. Roberta had been drinking steadily during their absence and was half drunk. She was still lying on the bed, wiggling her toes.

"What kept you?" she asked thickly.

"Sorry to keep you waiting," apologized McDevin, embracing Linda.

"Guess who's tellin' Canyon about the birds and bees?" questioned Crolley.

"Old horse face," said Roberta sullenly. "Bill called the old bitch up after you guys left. Boy, she makes me mad. She's so damned high and mighty, so goddamn patronizing. She's so good she makes me sick. Then the minute she thinks she's alone, she's worse than any of us."

"They make two of a kind," said Crolley. "Canyon is the same way. All the time he gives Mike and me holy hell for what he considers dangerously low morals, then he sneaks around and does the same thing himself."

"All that you say may be true," said McDevin, "but that doesn't help us find a place for everybody to sleep."

Linda had been silent all through this and had been looking hard at McDevin ever since he entered the room.

"Mike," she said, "pour me a stiff drink. I'm beginning to enjoy myself."

"Okay, sweetheart, say when," answered McDevin gayly. He grabbed a bottle from the dresser and found that it weighed surprisingly little.

"Hey," he protested. "What happened to our booze?"

"Well, I must confess," said Linda confidentially. "I had a few neat ones while you were gone and so did Roberta. As a matter of fact, we resolved our differences during your absence to the point where we are quite good friends."

"Well, I'm glad for that," said McDevin. "Never mind the whiskey. We haven't started on Crolley's bottle yet."

"Oh, but I'm afraid we have," said Linda. "We pinched a drink when the other bottle went dry. I put it back in his bag so I would have an opportunity to break the news to you gently."

McDevin pulled a bottle three-quarters full from Crolley's musette bag. "You gals really lap it up when you start, don't you?"

"Especially somebody else's whiskey," said Crolley. "But, since you girls are so pretty, and such sweet young things, we'll let you get by with it this time. As a matter of fact, I think I'll have a drink with you. Mike, while you're at it, give me a couple of fingers."

"I'm stinking," said Roberta, "but pour me one, too. While you're at it, give me a whole hand."

"Hell, we're on our last bottle," protested McDevin. "How about settling for three fingers?"

"Three fingers and a thumb and you're on," said Roberta.

McDevin filled four glasses halfway. "I'll be completely neutral about this thing," he said. "I'll give everybody three fingers."

"You'll be shy two," giggled Linda. "Four times three is twelve, you know, and you only have ten digits. Funny, isn't it?"

"Laugh, I thought I'd die," said Roberta.

McDevin handed the glasses around, held his glass on high, and said, "Here's to it, let's do it, there's nothing to it, even though you'll rue it."

"We have a poet in our midst," said Roberta, and she drank her whiskey with a relish.

"And a very nice poet, I'd say," said Linda.

"He smells," said Crolley.

"He smells beautiful," said Linda.

McDevin grabbed Linda in his arms and kissed her softly on the lips. "You're sweet, darlin'," and he kissed her long and deep.

"Are you goin' to sit there like a dunce," Roberta asked Crolley, "or are you goin' to rape me like a man?"

"You mean I've got a choice?" inquired Crolley. "Why don't you rape me? I rape easy."

"I'm a pushover myself," answered Roberta. She got up from

123

the bed, put her glass on the dresser and came back to the middle of the room. "I'm gettin' tired of foolin' around," she announced, and she removed her unbuttoned shirt. "I'm going to get in bed," she said. "I'm twenty-four years old, ready, willing, and able. I'm only goin' to occupy half the bed and if anybody wants to join me, he's welcome."

"Don't be so crude," said Crolley.

"Look who's talkin'," said McDevin in surprise. "You've been so damn eager all night you almost threw a rod. Now that you have a chance, why don't you take it?"

"Okay," said Crolley, "But what are you going to do? I'll be damned if I'll let you watch."

"We don't intend to watch," said McDevin. "We'll turn off the light and sit over in the chair."

"Yeah, but you'll listen," protested Crolley. "Why don't you take Linda in the bathroom? The tub's big."

"You go to hell, Dick," answered McDevin. "When you get done, it's our turn."

"Wait a minute," said Linda. "You have a regular time-table set up, haven't you? I haven't consented to sleep with you. All I want to do is drink." She moved toward the dresser where she poured herself a small portion of whiskey.

"Okay, baby," said McDevin. "We'll sit in the chair for awhile, and later on you can get in bed with Roberta, and Dick and I will sleep on the floor."

Linda skipped lightly to the door to switch off the light, then she made her way back to McDevin. He kissed her quickly and led her to the big chair underneath the floor lamp and pulled her down on his lap once again.

"You're wonderful, Linda," said Mike.

"It's only the spirits that prompt you to say that," said Linda coyly. "If you were sober it would be a different story."

"No, I have decided that actually I am very fond of you. I'm serious, darling. Ever since that first night in Cambridge I've known it, but I wouldn't admit it until now." He held her more tightly and pressed his lips to hers.

"I want another drink," said Linda and rose to her feet. She got the bottle, poured her glass one quarter full and drank deeply.

The liquor had begun to tell on Linda and she swayed ever so slightly on her beautiful legs. She emptied her glass. Methodically, she removed her dress and laid it gently in McDevin's lap. He sat there, open-mouthed, staring at her in the faint light seeping in through the closed blind. She took off her shoes from her stockingless feet and placed them neatly under the bed. With deft fingers, she removed her brassière and, with equal adroitness, dropped her black panties to the floor. Linda turned around silently, displaying her exquisite body. Her breasts were round, and hard. Her waist was small and elegant. Long legs and thighs expanded to round, well-shaped hips.

"I'm yours, Mike," she whispered. "Say that you like me."

"I—I—what I mean to say is, of course, I like you! I think you're beautiful!"

Linda kissed McDevin, then turned suddenly and walked into the bathroom.

"I'll be out in a minute," she called over her shoulder.

McDevin got up quickly from his chair and walked to the bed. Over the protest of Crolley and Roberta, he took two blankets and two pillows and by the time Linda came out of the bathroom he had them spread out on the floor.

"Slip in here, darling," he said.

"I'll do no such thing," she said. "I simply wanted you to see how beautiful I am."

An ominous knock sounded on the door. It sounded again, persistently. "I'm fast asleep," Roberta said. There was a look of stark terror in Linda's eyes. McDevin said in a stage whisper, "Put your dress on, quick."

"Don't get excited," said Crolley aloud. "Let's find out who it is. Maybe it's Mildred."

"You find out," said McDevin. "It's your idea."

Linda and Roberta slipped on their outer garments and, by mutual agreement, hid their underthings in the lower drawer of the dresser. In the meantime, Crolley and McDevin gathered the pillows and blankets from the floor, put them back into place, and then jumped into bed. Linda and Roberta ran to the bathroom and closed the door. It was like clockwork. No one gave directions, but all the parts seemed to fall into place. The knock increased in intensity and sounded more and more impatient.

"Who is it?" croaked Crolley.

"Open up! Open up!" demanded the voice from without.

"Who is it?" repeated Crolley.

"Never mind. Open up!" said the voice.

"I never let strange men in my room," said Crolley, attempting to be facetious.

"That won't do you any good," said McDevin. "Get up and let them in."

"You get up and let them in," said Crolley.

"You're closer to the door," said McDevin.

"If you want them in, get up and let them in," said Crolley. "I'm staying right here."

"Okay, coward," said McDevin. He got up and opened the door.

In the doorway stood a slender, impeccably dressed, middle-aged man. It was the night manager of the Cumberland Hotel. He gestured elegantly as he strode into the room.

"What, may I ask, is going on here?"

"We're trying to get some sleep," said Crolley. "We're war heroes, trying to rest."

"We have reliable information," said the middle-aged man precisely, "which indicates that there are unscrupulous goings-on in this room, and I mean to get to the bottom of it."

"There's nothing going on in here," lied Crolley. His face was a mask of innocence.

"Not a damn thing," echoed McDevin.

"None the less, there were female voices emanating from this room, and I, as night manager, intend to determine their origin and deprive you of your rooms as violators of His Majesty's law."

"There've been no female voices from this room," said Crolley lamely. "Maybe my friend talks in his sleep. He has a falsetto voice. He used to be a choirboy."

"Never mind," ordered the night manager. "I must ask you to leave."

"What the hell for?" asked McDevin. "There are no women here."

"I have reliable reports that there were," said the hotel manager.

"Well, look for yourself," said Crolley. "There are no women here. How can there be female voices when there are no women?"

"There is something in what you say," admitted the manager.

"Well, just search the place," suggested McDevin. "Look under the bed and in the closets." Then he added boldly, "Check the bathroom while you're at it. Then get the hell out of here."

The manager was silent and then admitted reluctantly, "Perhaps I've wronged you gentlemen. Please accept my apologies on behalf of the Cumberland Hotel. I hope you realize," he continued, "that we have to be most careful these days, what with the war and all. If you will excuse me, I'll retire. Sorry if I caused by any inconvenience."

"You did," said McDevin coldly. "Good-night."

The middle-aged man strode out into the corridor and down towards the elevator. McDevin watched him to make sure he didn't return and then closed the door and locked it.

"All clear," he said. Linda and Roberta emerged from the bathroom.

"We'd better be quiet," said Crolley. "Or we're going to get thrown out of here."

"I bet that goddamn Mildred turned us in," said Roberta. "That's the way she is. 'Don't do as I do, do as I say.' "

Linda removed her dress and stood naked again. Without a word McDevin laid a blanket on the floor and two pillows.

"Let's flip for the bed," said Crolley.

"That's the smartest thing you've said all night, Dick," said McDevin. "Do you want to match or call it?"

"You flip and I'll call it," answered Crolley. "But let's be honest about it, sonny boy. I can't tell a head from a tail on these British half-crown pieces."

"Call it," said McDevin as he flipped a coin.

"Head," said Crolley.

McDevin exposed the coin and called Roberta over to verify it. She sighed and said to Crolley, "Okay, lucky, get down on the floor."

"I never do win the toss with that bastard," said Crolley. "I should have known better."

CHAPTER

9

CYNTHIA WALLACE WALKED SWIFTLY AND EFFICIENTLY DOWN the hall, humming gaily to herself, happy with the world and her station in it. She was a hotel maid like her mother before her, and already she had three years at the Cumberland. She was making six pounds a week in addition to an equal sum that was given her as tips from generous Americans, or picked up from the rooms of careless patrons. She was waking the guests, and of all the things about her job, she liked that best. It was very interesting to her the way some people slept; and sometimes, in the case of American guests, she found paramours. It was a source of great amusement to her when the manager threw them out. And it was funnier yet when the guests and their illicit bed companions would plead and beg her not to report them. Sometimes, they even offered to bribe her with money. And whenever they did, she took it.

She giggled, and that thrilling, prickly feeling that accompanies goose pimples ran up and down her spine, as she thought of the American lieutenant who had seduced her. She wished more of them would try. If they would, she would show the proper amount of resistance, yield with apparent reluctance, and then, after it was over, sob softly and say that her chastity had been violated against her will. Then she would mention her "husband," although she wasn't actually married. The sympathetic boobs would offer her a pound or two, or maybe even five. It was really a form of prostitution, she admitted, but it wasn't like standing on Piccadilly and advertising it, or having rooms and laying the boys as they came along. After all, what with the hardships of war, she felt that she deserved the extra money she could make.

This morning, she thought, was a grand time for seduction. She wished now that she had run more slowly when the American officer had chased her yesterday around the corridor. If he hadn't given up so quickly, she thought, she'd be a pound or two ahead by now, maybe—at least, she'd be satisfied. Perhaps he would be among the guests she would awaken this morning, she wondered hopefully. He'd be sure to try again. She shivered in anticipation. Any man who would chase her around the corridor, would be bound to give her a good go. Oh, this *was* a happy day.

She inserted her key in the lock of 801 and opened the door. She went straight to the window and drew the broad, dark, velvet blackout curtain. When she turned around, she gasped in astonishment. There before her were not only two in bed, but also two on the floor. They were all breathing heavily, sound asleep. This was rich, she thought. She moved stealthily nearer and looked more closely. She gasped again, for there on the floor, lying beside a very attractive blond young lady was the young chap who had pursued her unsuccessfully the day before. She walked quietly to the door and closed it noiselessly—debating what to do. Mr. Godfrey, the manager, was capable of being quite disagreeable with guests on such occasions. He always rewarded her with kind words, praise and promise of advancement. But unfortunately, to date, these promises had never been consummated, nor did kind words and praise put money in her pocket. On the other hand, since there were four of them, and since there were three American uniforms scattered here and there about the room, perhaps the occupants would be inclined to bribe her for silence. She was in the midst of great cogitation concerning the subject when McDevin, subconsciously aware that someone had invaded the room, awoke with a start. He looked at Cynthia dumbly as if trying to comprehend the situation. Suddenly cognizant of the presence of a naked woman by his side, the preceding night's activities came back to him like a flash. Regret and shame surged through his body. He felt like running away. Then he considered Linda's delicious body and his sense of possession came over him so strongly that his impulse to get away subsided.

"Beautiful day," he said blandly. "What time is it?"

" 'Alf past nine," answered Cynthia.

"Be a good girl and hand me a cigarette, will you? Help yourself."

Cynthia obliged, taking a pack from the dresser and handing it with matches to McDevin.

"This is all very improper," said Cynthia reprovingly. "I should report you immediately to Mr. Godfrey."

"Who's he?" asked McDevin with forced nonchalance, lighting his cigarette as he spoke.

" 'E's the manager," answered Cynthia. " 'E can be nasty at times like these, 'e can," she warned. "I shouldn't relish being in your shoes."

"You mean you're going to turn us in?" asked McDevin.

"It's the thing to do," answered Cynthia with all the righteousness she could muster.

McDevin was silent as he pondered his predicament. Cynthia waited.

"Look around and see if you can find a drink for me. I need some hair of the dog that bit me."

"Beg your pardon?" inquired Cynthia.

"I'm hungover," explained McDevin. "I drank too much Scotch last night and now I feel bad. I'll be much better if I have another drink."

"I see," said Cynthia, checking the empty bottles. "These containers are dry," she continued. "But 'er's a glass that's 'alf full."

"Well, I'll tell you what you do," said McDevin, attempting some apple-polishing tactics. "You pour half of it in another glass for yourself and give me what's left."

"Oh, I couldn't possibly," said Cynthia. "It's against the rules. I'd be sacked for sure."

"Who'd find out?" inquired McDevin.

"Someone would smell it."

"Not if you'd smoke a cigarette and chew some gum."

"Well—all right," said Cynthia dubiously. "Provided you 'ave the gum."

"A whole pocketful," said McDevin. "Go ahead," he urged. "Thrown it down."

Cynthia divided the remaining Scotch and, giving McDevin his glass, she lifted her own, said, "Cheers," and drank it all. McDevin did likewise.

"That's very good," said Cynthia. "We can't get it, you know. You Americans 'ave all the money."

"I feel better already," declared McDevin.

"Your friends sleep soundly," said Cynthia, taking McDevin's glass and setting it with her own on the dresser.

"They seem to," answered McDevin. "But we were all pretty

well boozed-up last night before we went to bed. You'll find some gum in the pocket of my blouse, hanging over there on the chair. You'd better chew some before you report us to your boss or he'll smell liquor on your breath. I'd get it for you, but I haven't any clothes on as you can probably guess."

"I shouldn't mind," said Cynthia suggestively, fluttering her eyelashes.

"Yeah, but I would," said McDevin.

"I see," said Cynthia coldly. "I ain't good enough for you." She started for the door.

"Of course, you're good enough for me," said McDevin hastily, "but it would be embarrassing for both of us if somebody awoke and I was trotting around here in front of you naked. Besides, if you want to be loved, you got the wrong boy. The guy on the floor is your man."

Cynthia hesitated, then turned on McDevin in virtuous indignation. "Who said anything about going to bed," she almost shouted. "A decent girl isn't safe, nowadays. I'll 'ave you know I wouldn't crawl in bed with the likes of you for a thousand pounds."

"I'll do it for free," came Roberta's voice from the floor. "What time is it?"

"About a quarter of ten, I guess," said McDevin.

"Too bad," said Roberta. "Missed it again. Oh, well, another day, another dollar. Guess I'll have to wait till tomorrow."

"Why don't you take the afternoon train?" suggested Mike.

"I'd never get untangled with little John here in time," said Roberta. "Besides, I've got a policy never to take afternoon trains when I can take one the next morning."

Cynthia cleared her throat.

"Oh, excuse me," apologized McDevin. "This is—you didn't tell me your name."

"It's Cynthia," she said after a pause.

"Oh," said McDevin. "This is Cynthia. She's going to turn us in to the manager."

"Have fun," said Roberta.

"You're bloody well right I'm going to turn you in," cried Cynthia, abashed by the apparent unconcern of McDevin and Roberta. "What 'e won't do to you. It won't be very pleasant."

"I believe you," said McDevin. "I believe you."

Cynthia's eyes narrowed.

"On second thought," she said patronizingly. "I'd 'ate to see you people out in the street. Perhaps I could be persuaded to forget it for a few quid."

"Quid? That's a fish, isn't it," asked McDevin.

"You got the idea," said Roberta. "It means she's playing you for a sucker. A few quid means a few pounds."

"I see," mused McDevin. "I'm damned near out of quid, but old Dick has a pocketful. Everytime there's been a check to pay he's been some place else. Why don't you reach into his blouse, Roberta, and give me his wallet? It's in his inside pocket."

"Not me," protested Roberta. "I'm not about to go through a man's pockets. If you want to give her his dough, get it yourself."

"But I'm not dressed," said McDevin.

"Well, if she hasn't seen a naked man before," said Roberta, "it's time she got a good look at one."

"I'll 'ide my eyes," volunteered Cynthia.

"I'll bet," said Roberta with sarcasm. "Do't be so damned modest, Mike."

"Well, okay, here goes," said McDevin with resignation. And he got out of bed carefully so that he wouldn't wake Linda. He took five pounds from Crolley's wallet, handed it to Cynthia, then climbed back in bed.

"Thank you," she said. And looking once again at McDevin, she opened the door and withdrew.

"She'll probably tell the manager anyway," said McDevin. "The old bitch."

"They never have before," said Roberta.

"You mean you have been in this predicament before?" asked McDevin in surprise.

"Only in England," answered Roberta.

"Sex is a very essential part of your life, isn't it, Roberta?" asked McDevin seriously. "To you, sleeping with a man is a sort of every-day thing, isn't it?"

"Every night, too," said Roberta. "And why not? It's a very natural thing, as far as I'm concerned."

"I know," admitted McDevin, "but where is your sense of value? If you ever get married, what is your husband going to think about your Bohemian attitude?"

"I don't give a damn," answered Roberta. "If he doesn't like me this way, he won't have to marry me. A nurse can always make a living."

"Yeah, but suppose you fall in love?" continued McDevin. "And suppose that the guy you fall in love with doesn't want to marry you because you're not a virgin?"

"I've been in love," said Roberta. "Dozens of times. Besides, I'll cross that bridge when I come to it."

"Well, it's none of my business," sighed McDevin. "I wish we had a drink."

Linda opened her eyes and looked at McDevin. She stretched herself indulgently and sat up in bed. She ran her slender fingers through her hair and then reached down and kissed Mike lightly on the lips and said, "Good morning, darling."

"Good morning, sleepyhead. I thought you'd never wake up."

"Anybody hungry?" McDevin asked. "I'm starved."

"I'll buy that," said Roberta. She moved away from the sleeping Crolley and got up.

Linda rose, too, and stretched herself again and moved her lithe body with effortless ease to the bathroom and closed the door. McDevin gazed at Roberta, and said, "Let's wake up Crolley."

Roberta began gathering together her clothes. "How do you wake him up?"

"He always sleeps like this when he's been drinking," said McDevin. "When we are back at the base, Canyon usually beats on a coal pail and sings *Black Magic*."

"Well, it's unique, anyhow," said Roberta, hooking her brassière. "Aren't you going to get dressed?"

"Yeah, I guess I better," answered McDevin, and he got out of bed. He knelt down beside Crolley and shook him vigorously. "Wake up deadhead, the world's on fire." He shook him again and repeated, "Wake up, wake up, rise and shine, hit the deck." Crolley stirred, then opened his eyes. He sat up slowly, then lay down again.

"Santa Maria," he muttered sleepily. "Boy, this floor is hard!"

"Get up," said McDevin. "It's 'way past ten o'clock."

"Where's Roberta?" asked Crolley.

"Standing right in front of you."

Crolley looked up. "I didn't recognize you, darling. Come back in bed."

"Not now," said McDevin. "We gotta get up and get out of here. I bribed the maid with five pounds from your wallet so that she wouldn't report us, but I don't know how long she's good for."

"If it's my five pounds," said Crolley, "she better be good forever. What's the idea, anyhow?"

"Well I paid all the bills last night," said McDevin, "and I thought it was your turn for a change."

"I'll argue with you later," said Crolley. "Get back in bed, Roberta."

"Let's eat first," she said. "I'm starving."

"Who can think of food at a time like this?" asked Crolley. "But if you insist, I'll sacrifice and drag these tired bones out of bed." He pulled himself slowly to his feet.

Linda emerged from the bathroom and crawled back into bed. "It's nice here," she said. "I think I'll stay awhile."

"You too?" asked McDevin. "Everybody wants to stay, including me. But I'm afraid if we don't dress and get out of here, the management is going to catch us. I've paid off one maid already this morning, but there are going to be more, soon, to change the bed."

"Always the practical one, aren't you?" said Crolley.

"Oh, they don't come until nearly noon," said Linda. McDevin looked at her quickly, but remained silent.

Roberta went into the bathroom and Crolley began to dress. McDevin stood motionless for a moment, then looked long and hard at the beautiful Linda and crawled in bed beside her.

"Oh, no! None of that," objected Crolley. "You wouldn't let Roberta and me, so I'm not going to let you."

"Please, Dick," pleaded Linda. "Take Roberta and leave. I want to talk to Mike seriously. We'll be away from here in an hour and by that time you will be done with your breakfast and you can have the room for the rest of the day if you like."

She was so sincere in her plea that Crolley consented. Within ten minutes he and Roberta were dressed and had left the room.

After they had gone, Linda got up and bolted the door and then crawled back in bed and snuggled close to McDevin. "I want you, Mike."

"I don't understand you," said Mike. "In Cambridge you begged me not to, but now that you are here, you can't seem to get enough."

"I might as well tell you," she confessed, "that I'm in love with you, and I want you while I can get you. If you don't get killed in the war, you will go back to your wife, and I lose you either way. I want to sleep with you every chance I get."

"You shouldn't love me . . ." began Mike.

"I know that," interrupted Linda. "Don't lecture me, please. I know I'm wrong and I'm a fool. Don't remind me of it. Just make love to me Mike—now."

* * *

McDevin and Crolley sat in the first-class compartment of a tiny English train, headed for Long Melford where they would catch a truck back to the base. Another night had passed in the Cumberland. It was more of the same thing, liquor and sex. The only difference was that Crolley had registered for another room to avoid sleeping on the floor. Roberta had missed the train again, and was at the station to kiss them both good-by. Linda had departed for Cambridge that morning. Mildred had gone the day previous, bringing Roberta's luggage to 801, and Bill Canyon, still piqued at his two cohorts for their ill-timed invasion of his room, cut his pass a day short.

"Boy, I sure hate to go back," griped Crolley. "Roberta is one in a million. And so far as I'm concerned, London is one hot town."

"I'll agree with the first part of your statement," said Mc-Devin, "but I'm afraid we both are unqualified to express an honest opinion about London. All we saw of it was a hotel room and a couple of bars."

"What more could you ask for?" asked Crolley. "Sex and liquor. What would the world be without them?"

"Probably better off."

"What are you so down in the dumps about, lover boy? Linda was even better looking than Roberta. And last night you had more to drink than I did."

"All that glitters is not gold," warned McDevin. "I got troubles, bad troubles."

"I told you to take a pro," said Crolley.

"Oh, my God, Dick, don't you ever think of anything else except sex? No matter what we talk about, you either have to bring booze or women into it."

"What's wrong with that? As far as I'm concerned, that's all I care to talk about."

"Don't you ever want to make anything out of yourself? You know, we might get out of this thing alive. When we get back to the States, don't you want to do something worth while? You have to eat, you know, and you have to work to eat."

"You're so right," agreed Crolley, "but I figure I might just as well do something I like. It's easier that way."

"Give me a for instance."

"Oh, I thought I might play a piano in a whorehouse."

"Be serious, you damn fool," said McDevin sharply.

"Like hell, I'll be serious," retorted Crolley. "I'm not even going to think about being serious until the day I'm back in the good old U. S. A. Until then I'm going to continue to be a damn fool and enjoy it. Now, how about unloading those big troubles. Maybe I could make you feel better."

"I don't think anyone could make me feel better," confessed McDevin. "It's one of those things you just have to sweat out." He hesitated, then added, "Linda's in love with me."

"How do you know?" asked Crolley.

"She told me," stated McDevin. "And I don't know whether I'm happy or sad about it."

"If that's all you're worrying about," laughed Crolley, "forget it. I bet she hasn't told that to more than a hundred guys in the last thirty days. Hell, she's seen you only a half a dozen times. How could she know whether she's in love with you or not? If you ask me, she's playing you for a sucker."

"I don't think so. I really believe she's serious."

"Nuts. I'll bet you she's just trying to take you for all she can get out of you."

"I haven't spent over twenty pounds on her and she's never asked me for a dime. Besides, I think that she's relatively well heeled. What I mean is, she's got a job, and that apartment of hers is nicely furnished and, considering the rations over here, she wears fairly decent clothes. No, I think you're wrong, Dick. If she wanted anything out of me, she would have asked me for it while we were in London."

"Well, did you ever stop to think, you big stoop," argued Crolley, "that maybe she'd like a free boatride to America and United States citizenship? Even as dumb as I am, I can see that there's going to be economic chaos in England when all this fighting is over, and she's nobody's fool."

"That's no argument. She knows I'm married. I'm not about to divorce Katherine, and I told her so."

"Well, goddamn it, what are you worried about then? Even if she is in love with you—so what? Let her love."

"I'm not built that way, Dick. Maybe you could do it, but I can't."

"Well, you should have thought of that before, you jackass."

"Well, hell, I didn't ask her to fall in love with me. What did you expect me to do, take her out and say, 'Don't fall in love with me'?"

"You don't have to come right out and tell them in so many words—just let them know, subtle-like."

"As I said before, I told her I was married the second time I saw her, and I've been wearing this wedding band all the time."

"Good God," sighed Crolley. "I still don't see what you're worried about. She walked into it with her eyes open. Why make yourself a nervous wreck over it? Just let it go. You don't have to see her again, you know."

"Look, Dick," said McDevin in desperation. "Suppose she's pregnant?"

"All right, suppose she is. You're a big boy now. Mike. If worse comes to worse, you know what to do about it."

"Not in England, I don't. Maybe back in Wyoming, but not in Merrie Ole England."

"Jeezis, McDevin, I didn't know you were so naive. I didn't mean for her to have an abortion; I meant blame it on somebody else."

"Who?" answered McDevin.

"Hell, anybody," said Crolley in some irritation. "They can't prove you're to blame. How do you know how many guys she's slept with? You crazy lame brain," continued Crolley, warming to his subject, "even if she *is* pregnant, how do you know that it's you who is responsible for it?"

"Oh, I wouldn't know for sure," said McDevin, "but she did say she wanted something to remember me by."

"McDevin," sighed Crolley with deep pity, "ever since the first day I met you, I have considered you to be of above average intelligence. When the occasion calls for it, you are suave and a man of the world. I have accepted your advice in almost every case. You have displayed, up until now, a surprising amount of common sense, but apparently, with all these good qualities, you lack one necessary garnishment—brains. So she wants *you* to get her pregnant, does she? Six times she's seen you, and she wants you to get her pregnant, even though she knows you're married. She loves you so much that she wants to bring your bastard child into the world. Now ain't that ducky! And you, you fathead, believe it. Did it ever occur to you that maybe she's already pregnant by another guy and wants to stick you? Or did it ever occur to you that, once she had your baby, she could always hold it over your head? And did it ever occur to you that, if you get her pregnant, she'd keep working on you until you divorced your wife? Goddamn, you're dumb!" When McDevin didn't answer Crolley said impatiently. "Look, let's forget the whole damn thing. We have a war to fight. By this time tomorrow we'll be on our way home from another mission. Let's talk about something pleasant while we have the opportunity."

"I guess you're right," admitted McDevin. "How about pulling that bottle of Scotch out of your musette bag and let's have a drink."

CHAPTER

10

A T TWO O'CLOCK THE NEXT MORNING MC DEVIN AND CROLLEY, at the insistence of an adamant charge of quarters, reluctantly pulled their tired bodies from bed. Canyon was already up. He had grown strangely cooler with each successive mission and, although he seemed to be friendly and in high spirits while on pass, he had become almost hostile, now that they were back on the base. This morning he didn't even wait to go to breakfast with his pals and crew members. Rather, with hardly a word, he dressed quickly and went on by himself. Crolley and McDevin were at a loss to explain his strange actions, but because of the seriousness of combat it was comparatively unimportant to them.

They learned the disagreeable news that the bomb load was light and the gasoline tanks were topped off, and, true to Crolley's prediction that "this will probably be a son of a bitch," the group was scheduled to bomb a target at Magdeburg, Germany, a town about fifty miles east southeast of Berlin, heavily defended by antiaircraft and enemy fighter planes.

The 487th Bomb Group began taking off from its station at about five o'clock. Two hours later they were in the bomber stream, flying toward the North Sea. They entered Germany from the north through a flak corridor just east of Cuxhaven, passing just out of range of the antiaircraft installations at Bremerhaven. The initial point was 320 degrees from the target, and they were favored with a forty-five-nautical-mile-per-hour tail wind at 24,000 feet. They were under continuous fighter attack from a spot midway between Bremen and Hamburg, until they reached the target itself, when the bandits ceased their offensive to avoid their own antiaircraft. It was after the initial point, and McDevin had picked up the target in his bombsight, that an FW 190, attacking from six o'clock, seriously damaged their B-17. They were in immediate danger. Intense flak was just ahead, and Canyon was finding it difficult to keep his altitude, despite the fact that he was pulling full power. Number four engine was almost knocked out, and number two engine was running rough. They were flying number three position in the low squadron.

When McDevin dropped the bomb load, momentarily the aircraft found it easier to maintain its altitude. Almost immediately, however, they were struck again. The intense flak had proved to be most accurate and Canyon was forced to drop from formation. It was impossible to keep up and they fell behind the bomber stream. Being crippled, they would be easy targets for the enemy fighters, lying in wait just outside the flak area, but the allied escort aircraft were sufficiently effective to prevent further attack there on the wounded ship.

"How far is it to friendly territory, Crolley?" Canyon asked over the interphone.

"It's about two hundred and thirty-six miles to Brussels, straight in. According to this morning's brief, that's the best place to head for. Think we can make it that far?"

"I don't know," answered Canyon. "We're about to lose number four and number two is runnin' rough. We're leaking oil pretty bad and I can't seem to get full power out of my other engines. I'm afraid we're going to have to lose some altitude. How's the flak between here and Brussels?"

Crolley regarded his maps with the flak areas drawn in. "We have to cross the Rhine yet and there's always flak boats there. We're bound to get shot at. With deviations in headings, we can manage to miss most other antiaircraft areas except those near Dusseldorf and Cologne. You can head in that direction and I'll try to steer you around the worst of it. With that forty-five-knot wind, you had better take up a heading of two-hundred-and-ninety-seven degrees."

"Roger," answered Canyon.

"Bombardier to crew," said McDevin. "Let's have another oxygen check."

The crew complied, and then McDevin admonished everybody to be on the lookout for enemy aircraft and to conserve ammunition as much as possible, since they would be within easy range of the fighters from the Munster and Cassel areas.

This was the most serious situation the crew had ever experienced. They knew they would either have to bail out or crash-land, and they were an easy target for enemy action because they were without protection from the formation. They knew, too, that, as time went on, they would lose altitude and thereby be easier to hit for the Kraut antiaircraft gunners. Within a short period of time, number four engine went out completely. Canyon was unable to feather the prop and its windmilling produced extra drag on the airplane, thereby increasing the fuel consumption. Despite their predicament, however, every crew member performed nobly. Crolley guided them expertly. McDevin directed the gunners, and Canyon, who had taken over the first pilot's job when Hal Barton had finished his missions, and a new co-pilot drew from all their knowledge and training to get the most out of the airplane.

Except for light flak, when they skirted antiaircraft areas, the flight progressed without serious interference from the enemy. Near Cologne they picked up a flight of three P-51's, which stayed close to them, except in flak regions, until they crossed the Rhine. They had continued gradually to lose altitude until they neared Maastricht, Belgium. They were at five thousand feet. Canyon and his new co-pilot were trying desperately to keep the aircraft aloft until they were nearer Brussels and in friendly territory. Once in allied-held land, they could bail out or crash-land in relative safety. They didn't relish landing in enemy territory, even though the *Wehrmacht* was on the run. If they were apprehended by "Jerry," they would more than likely be shot, since he was desperate now, and couldn't afford to take care of prisoners.

"How far away from the lines now, Crolley?" asked Canyon.

"About fifty miles," answered Crolley. "If you keep on your present heading, we'll come out just north of Brussels. We'd be a hell of a lot better off if we could get at least that far."

"We'll be damned lucky if we do," said Canyon. "We're losing altitude every minute."

"It'll take us about twenty-five minutes if we can keep up this ground speed," said Crolley. "Do your best, Bill."

"Pilot to crew," said Canyon crisply. "Prepare to bail out. I'm going to try to get this crate as close to Brussels as I can. You've got about twenty minutes to prepare. Check your parachutes and see that you have all the stuff you're supposed to have. You've all been briefed on how to do this and you've all expected to do it sometime or other, so just remember what you learned. Be sure to stay on interphone and don't leave the ship until I give the signal."

They struggled onward. In fifteen minutes they were over Louvain. Canyon warned the crew again.

"How about trying to crash-land it, Bill?" suggested Mike.

"Can't do it," came back Canyon. "Some of my controls are shot out, too. All right, everybody, you can see Brussels to your left. We just passed over the front line. When you hit the ground, head south and you'll probably be picked up by some British soldiers. When you get to Brussels go to the airfield there and report in to the RAF and they'll get you back to the base. 'Bye, 'bye, boys, it's been fun," and he rang the bail out signal.

The well-trained crew left the ship in an orderly fashion, plummeting toward the earth. Canyon was the last to leave. Beautiful, billowy, white parachutes carried them leisurely downward. Crolley and McDevin had left the ship almost at the same instant, and through pre-arranged plans they pulled their ripcords with the least possible delay, as soon as they had cleared the aircraft. They did this so that they would land close to each other and thereby avoid being on the ground alone. Ten minutes later they had reached the ground, within sight of each other. With the kind help of a north wind, they were at the very edge of the city of Brussels. After congratulating each other on the successful jump and deciding upon a plan of action, they began hiking toward the Brussels airfield. They could tell from the numerous C-47's that were flying overhead, making landing patterns, that the field was now in allied hands. They were thankful for many reasons. First of all, they were alive. Secondly, they were in allied territory. Thirdly, there was a possibility that when they arrived back in England, because of this mission, they would not be required to fly again, and perhaps they could go home. Although they had been through hell the past few hours, they had lost none of their spirit.

"I'm glad we're not in the RAF," said Crolley, as they trudged toward a road that apparently led to the city.

"Why?" asked McDevin.

"Well, there are not so many of them as there are of us," answered Crolley, "and when they get shot down or bail out and get back safely, they have to keep on flying. But with us, we have a chance of going home now."

"I'm just thankful we're alive," said McDevin. "I'm still shaking."

"I've got the palsy myself," admitted Crolley.

142

"I've been praying ever since we left Magdeburg," said McDevin. "And the Old Man came through."

"I suppose you think you got a corner on this praying market," said Crolley. "I said a few thousand words myself."

"Maybe I sound corny," said McDevin, "but now that the Lord answered our prayers, I think the least we can do is kneel down and say, 'Thank you.'"

"I'll buy that," agreed Crolley. "Where do we kneel?"

"Let's kneel right here," said McDevin.

"You lead off," said Crolley. "The Lord and I have a mutual understanding. He knows I'm not much good at this praying business, but he gets the idea."

"Well, instead of saying a prayer out loud, let's each say a silent prayer. I'd like that better."

The two young officers bowed their heads and gave thanks to God for their safety and very lives. Crolley was the first to get to his feet. In a moment McDevin joined him, and they continued walking. Neither of them spoke for several minutes.

"I think it's time for a drink," suggested Crolley.

"You think right," said McDevin, "but where are we going to get it?"

"Like I keep telling you," said Crolley, "navigators, being of superior intellect, never fall short. You seem to have forgotten a very salient bit of poop."

McDevin brightened. "Hell, yes, I remember! It's that little flask you carry!"

"You guessed it, my boy," said Crolley, as he withdrew a small metal flask from a zippered pocket of his flying suit. "My staff of life." He unscrewed the top and handed the bottle to McDevin. "Mike, since you are my best friend and partner in crime, I'm going to be generous and let you drink first. But be careful, chum, the thing only holds a half pint. Leave some for me."

McDevin laughed and took the flask. He gave Crolley a friendly cuff on the head and drank deeply, then handed the flask back.

"Without a doubt," said McDevin, "that was absolutely the best drink of whiskey that I have ever had."

"I agree with you," said Crolley, as he took the flask away from his lips. "I filled this thing before we left the States and promised myself I'd never open it except on an occasion such as this. Brother, such an occasion! Want another one before I put it away?"

"I do," said McDevin, "but let's save it." Crolley put the flask back in his pocket and the two began walking again. Within a very short period of time they reached the main road for which they were heading and began following it toward Brussels. They hadn't gone far when they were picked up by a British reconnaissance car which took them directly to RAF headquarters at the Brussels airfield.

They were received coldly by the British who, after listening to their story, refused to feed them, but sent a report by wireless to SHAEF headquarters in England. They were told to report to the field every morning until transportation could be arranged to take them back to England. The two hitched a ride into the deliriously happy, liberated city in a car driven by a uniformed Belgium woman who dropped them off, at their request, in front of the Metropole Hotel.

The two Americans looked odd in their electrical flying suits, but they were recognized as allies by the Belgians, who crowded around them in the street and kissed them. These people had been under the yoke of Nazism for years. They were joyous to the point of hysteria, having got rid of the German scourge only the previous day. McDevin and Crolley made their way toward the entrance of the beautiful hostelry. McDevin sometimes dragged Crolley, since the latter was prone to take advantage of the attractive, jubilant girls.

"For God's sake, come on, Dick. Let's go inside and get some rooms. You can make the girls later."

"Killjoy," accused Crolley, as he kissed one more. "Wish I knew what they were saying."

"What difference does it make?" said McDevin. "Come on."

"Well, hell," protested Crolley. "Maybe they're asking me to do something I want to do. These girls are very friendly and I am an ambassador of good will."

"Well, you don't smell like one," said McDevin, and they walked into the lobby of the hotel. It was a corridor actually, with the lobby over to the right and a kind of sitting-room on the left. Crolley and McDevin walked up to the desk. McDevin began to speak lamely in French.

"I can speak English, m'sieur," said the hotel clerk with a smile. "What is it you wish?"

"We'd like a room," said Crolley. "With blondes and brunettes."

"You are Americans!" the clerk almost shouted, and he hurried away busily, returning almost immediately with a pudgy little man who sported a bald pate. He fairly gushed all over them and spoke in a mixture of French and English.

"What's he talking about?" asked Crolley. "All I know is bedroom French."

"Well, the best I can make out," said McDevin, "is that we are great guys and we can stay here for free."

"Take him up on it quick, before he changes his mind."

"Yeah. I'm going to. If I only knew what to say."

"Can't you nod your head or something?"

McDevin smiled at the little man and said with his best French accent, *Merci, m'sieur, merci."* The pudgy little man took them to their rooms personally, talking incessantly with many dramatic gestures. He even stopped to kiss them both on the cheek. When he mentioned the word *Wehrmacht* he scowled and spat.

"This bird is a character, isn't he?" said Crolley. "Back in Springfield, we would throw him in the river—with weights, yet."

They were given suite number 611, composed of one large room and a magnificent bathroom. The fat little man extended more compliments and bowed out, leaving McDevin and Crolley by themselves, their disreputable appearance contrasting sharply with the richly appointed room.

"Oh, dear me," said Crolley. "I forgot my valet. I just don't know how I'll get along without him."

"Oh, shut up and let's take a bath. I'll take mine first."

"Like hell you will! I have never been addicted to baths, but after today I'm convinced I need one."

"Why change after so many years?" asked McDevin 'with sarcasm.

"I got scared today," answered Crolley.

"So what?" asked McDevin as he started to undress. "What's being scared got to do with taking a bath?"

"I guess my humor is too subtle for you," commented Dick, and he began to take off his clothes, hurriedly.

"Now, look," said McDevin. "This is no time to act like a

145

couple of kids. There's no need for you to race around trying to beat me into the bathroom. Sometimes I think you're nuts."

"For your information, I am nuts. I was just nutty enough to bring along a razor and some shaving soap. And I was also nutty enough to bring along that flask of whiskey. Which gives me an idea. Let's have a drink." And he pulled out the flask from his pocket.

McDevin poured the remaining whiskey into two glasses and they drank.

"You know, Uncle Sam is a very generous guy," said McDevin. "If he hadn't been farsighted enough to give us these escape kits, we'd be in a hell of a shape. As it stands now, we each have three thousand francs, which, if we are frugal, ought to last us until we get back to England."

"Hell, I didn't think of that," said Crolley, and he produced his escape kit from one of the many pockets in his flying suit. "You know, I've never opened one of these damn things before. I hope these francs are good. Hey, look at these pretty maps, Mike. What can we use these for?"

"They're just right for diapers, or maybe you can trap some pretty girl with them."

"From the looks of those girls when we came in, they don't need trapping."

McDevin went into the bathroom and began to draw his tub. Crolley, with his miniature shaving kit, followed him, and they began their ablution. McDevin was halfway through with a hot, luxurious, much-needed bath when he heard a scream. He peered from around the oil-silk curtains that surrounded the bathtub and said to Crolley, "What the hell's going on?"

"I was just tryin' out this thigamajig. This goddamn place ain't safe."

McDevin flopped back in the tub, overwrought with hilarious laughter. "That thingamajig," he exploded between gutffaws, "is a bidêt. What'd you do, sit down on it?"

"Yeah," admitted Crolley ruefully.

"And turned on the water?"

"Uh-huh, but I'd never used one before. Hurry up and get out of the bathtub."

After they both had bathed and shaved, they lay down naked on the twin beds in the bedroom and lighted cigarettes. They were

146

discussing the events of the day when the door of the room opened and a petite maid walked in. They both scrambled for cover.

"Hey, haven't you any respect for our modesty? Why don't you knock before you come in?" said Crolley.

She began babbling in French.

"What's she saying, Mike?"

"Something about being at our service," answered McDevin.

"Ask her if that includes stud service."

"Oh, don't be funny. That little bald fat fellow must have sent her up."

The maid began bustling around the room, picking up the filthy clothes that were scattered about, trying to restore some semblance of order in a room that had been completely disarranged, even though its occupants had been there but an hour.

"Hey, Maud, be careful what you do with those clothes. They're all we have. Tell her, Mike, before she walks out with them."

"Mademoiselle, parlez vous anglais?"

"I speak *anglais* very little." She gave them an effervescent smile.

"The clothes," said McDevin. "Leave them there."

"Oui," replied the maid, and she laid them down on the chair. "They are very dir-tee."

"I know they are dirty," said Crolley. "But we'd look silly running around here naked."

"Thank you very much," said McDevin.

"Oui," said the maid again, but made no effort to leave.

"We're prisoners," said Crolley. "She outflanked us. Why is it women are drawn to me so?"

"You can go now," said McDevin. "Go," and he gestured her away.

"I help you," said the maid. "Would you like champagne?"

"We don't need any help, but we would like some champagne," said Crolley. "Make her understand, Mike. Don't let her slip away."

Crolley got out of bed and wrapped a sheet around him and led the maid to the bathroom. "See that gadget?" he queried, pointing to the douche bowl. "It looks like a midget's wash-stand. Do they have these in every room?"

"She doesn't understand you, Dick. Why waste your time talking to her?"

"Listen, if I couldn't understand somebody and they showed me a bidêt, you can bet your sweet life I'd start understanding." Then he turned to the maid and pointed again to the bidêt. The maid walked over and turned on the water, then giggled and said, *"Comprende?"*

"Yeah, I get it," said Crolley. He went back to the bed. "Your witness, Mike."

"Mademoiselle," said McDevin. "Can you get us some cognac? *Comprende vous* cognac?"

"Oui, m'sieur, cognac. I get *beaucoup,"* and she bounded out of the room.

In five minutes she returned with two bottles of best quality cognac. It had *Wehrmacht* overprinted in red on the label.

"Looks like Jerry had to leave behind his libation," said Crolley. "Too bad."

"This is pretty good stuff," said McDevin, carefully perusing the label.

"I see you know your French well enough to read about booze," commented Crolley.

"Pour us a drink. I'm thirsty," said McDevin, ignoring Crolley's innuendo.

Crolley obeyed. "Why don't you get rid of that maid so I can take this goddamn sheet off?"

"Oh for . . . well, take it off, anyway, if it bothers you so goddamn much. You're not in the United States now. Over here in Belgium they take a different viewpoint. A maid is supposed to ignore stuff like that."

"Well, she can't ignore stuff like mine," said he, disrobing himself. "There, what do you think of that, Frenchy?"

The maid blushed.

"Fini," said McDevin. And the girl opened the door to go. She turned around and looked once more at Crolley, fluttered her eyelashes, and said, *"Voila!"* and closed the door.

"What did she mean, *voila?"* asked Crolley. "Don't tell me, I know. It's because I'm such an Adonis. Don't you wish you were an Adonis, Mike?"

"I don't give a damn," answered McDevin. "Let's 'Adonis' this drink and have another."

"In Springfield we castrate punsters at birth," said Crolley solemnly, and he gulped his drink.

Before long the two flyers had made a sizable hole in one bottle of cognac and were feeling very gay. The world was rosy and becoming brighter every minute. They lolled about the room, talking first about one thing and then another, when gradually they became conscious of a noise outside. Crolley went to the French doors that opened onto a balcony. The street was filled with people, happy Belgians who were celebrating their liberation, and who had gathered in such great numbers that the narrow street below looked like Times Square on New Year's Eve.

"Hey, Mike," said Crolley. "Come give a look at these people." He waved to the crowd below.

"What's down there?" asked McDevin.

"Like I told you, people, millions of people, singing and dancing and raisin' all kinds of hell."

"Well, somebody's goin' to start raisin' hell with you in a minute. I've got news for you."

"What's that?" asked Crolley absent-mindedly, intent on the scene below.

"You're standing out there without a stitch of clothes on."

Crolley turned around suddenly and ran with great speed across the room, his course coming to an end against a large, six-foot mirror by the doorway. He smacked it with a thud and staggered back groggily.

"You simple-minded bastard! Why in the hell did you do a thing like that?"

"I thought it was a door," said Crolley sheepishly.

"And where did you think the door led to?" asked McDevin sarcastically. And then he added, as an afterthought, "Did you hurt yourself?"

"Not much," answered Crolley, "but I saw stars for a minute."

"You know, Dick, I think this combat is gettin' the best of you. You do the silliest damn things at times."

"I'm tryin' for a Section Eight," said Crolley. "Let's get dressed and go eat. I suddenly realized something. Except for concentrated candy, we haven't eaten since two-thirty this morning."

McDevin readily agreed and they both put on their flying suits and underclothing, dirty as they were, and went downstairs to the dining room. They were treated royally by the manage-

149

ment and given the best of the sparse menu. They were served vintage champagne and strong black coffee.

Halfway through the meal, they were approached by a very attractive black-eyed brunette. She was tall and willowy and possessed poise, a combination usually lacking in run-of-the-mill European girls.

"How do you do? Are you Americans?" she asked.

Both Crolley and McDevin got up.

"Why, yes, we are," said McDevin.

"My name is Vera Lubin. I'm an American citizen."

"Indeed," said McDevin with doubt in his voice. "Won't you sit down and have some champagne?"

She assented and Crolley helped her with her chair.

"Thank you," she said, making herself comfortable. Then she continued, "My mother is Greek and my father is from New York. I was born in Manhattan. We were traveling when the war broke out and we got caught. We've been here nearly five years, as a matter of fact."

"Very interesting," said McDevin. "It's good to see you."

"What he means to say," said Crolley gallantly, "is that you are a very beautiful girl. Would you care to dine?"

"Yes, thank you, I would."

McDevin called the waiter over and Vera ordered.

"I heard that there were Americans in this hotel and came over right away. I thought I could help you. Besides, I wanted to be with my own kind, for a change. It's been a long time."

The girl went on to explain that her father was in the jewelry business and had extensive interests in the Netherlands. Her family had lived in relative comfort during the war and had been unsuspected by the Nazis. There was no doubting that she was an American, and as the meal progressed she became more and more friendly. She offered to exchange the invasion money in Crolley's and McDevin's escape kits, which, unbeknownst to the two flyers, was worthless. Just that day a new monetary system had come into being. She also invited them out to her house, but McDevin and Crolley declined and asked her to show them around Brussels instead.

After the meal was over she led them outside to the crowded streets. It was pitch black. Because of the danger of a Nazi air attack, there was complete blackout. The streets were still crowded with celebrating people and the three had to hold hands to keep from losing each other. Vera took them first to a little bar just around the corner from the Metropole Hotel. In the back were booths and a small place to dance. A three-piece orchestra played in European ragtime such numbers as *God Save the King, America,* and the *Star Spangled Banner* in honor of the liberating allied forces. McDevin, Crolley, and Vera drank cognac and red wine. They became pleasantly tight and Crolley tried his bedroom French out on nearly every girl in the place.

"*V'il a vous couchez avec moi?*" he asked. Some girls became belligerent, others didn't bother to answer, but a few consented. One woman in her middle thirties insisted that they start immediately. One drunken British soldier resented Crolley's intrusion and swung on him with a hard right and missed. The soldier was immediately taken away by British military police.

The next stop for the trio was a similar spot, larger, a few blocks away. When Vera passed around the word that she had Americans with her, the place was theirs. The cognac and champagne were free and McDevin and Crolley proceeded to take advantage of the situation.

After a while Crolley spotted a girl sitting alone at a far table, and went over to her. He sat down when the girl smiled at him. He was still there when McDevin and Vera decided to return to the hotel.

"Are you coming up to the room with me, Vera?" asked Mike.

"Why not?" she replied.

"Well, I just thought I had better ask you," said McDevin.

"I just said I'd go up," said Vera. "I didn't say I'd do anything else. Besides, I've got to phone my parents and tell them where I am. Have you got any liquor?"

"Yeah, we've got a fifth of cognac. Will that be enough?"

The two went up to 611. They opened the fifth of cognac and drank steadily for about an hour. Vera phoned her parents and told them where she was. "I'll be here all night," she said. "Of course, I'll be careful." Then she began talking in French.

After she had hung up, McDevin said, "Did you tell them you were going to stay all night with me?"

"Of course not," said Vera. "I told her I was staying with a friend. Don't forget my parents are from America, not from Belgium, and they haven't fully accepted the liberal ideas over here, even after five years."

"I'd better order another fifth of cognac," said McDevin. "Seems like all I've done since I've been here is drink, but I'm not really drunk yet." He called the desk for two more bottles, and then asked Vera, "What time is it?"

"One o'clock."

"My back! Do you call your folks so late at night?"

"Certainly, we never go to bed before one o'clock at our house, and we get up at ten. Besides, I'm twenty-three years old and I don't have to call them at all if I don't want to. Excuse me for a minute. I'd like to freshen up."

She was a tall girl and gave the impression of being unusually supple. She had coal-black hair, dark, shining eyes, and beautiful Semitic features. Her hair was long and hung down to her shoulders and her skin was smooth and clear. Her mouth was large and moist.

"You remind me of a girl I know in England," said Mike. "Her name is Linda Chambers. She's in love with me."

"That's too bad," said Vera. "Are you going to marry her?"

"I can't," answered McDevin. "I'm already married and I have a child."

"That always complicates matters, doesn't it?" said Vera. "Like I said, excuse me, I must freshen up," and she went into the bathroom, not bothering to close the door. She emerged shortly with fresh lipstick and newly combed hair. McDevin poured another drink. As they toasted each other, there was a loud knock at the door.

"You'd better hide somewhere, Vera," said McDevin. "I would hate to have them catch us together."

"You're not in the United States now, Mike. Things are different over here. They're not so narrow-minded. Go ahead and open the door."

Mike obeyed reluctantly. As he pulled the door open, a body fell in, stiff as a maple board, and hit the floor with a resounding thud. It was Crolley, stewed to the gills, and unconscious. McDevin was not surprised. It had happened before.

"I shouldn't have let him mix his drinks so much," commented McDevin, as he picked up Crolley and laid him on the bed.

"Looks to me like he can't take it," said Vera. "We drank as much as he did."

"There's where you're wrong," said Mike. "I know this guy pretty well. When he drinks he doesn't use sense. I'll venture to say he has drunk twice as much as you or I. If you remember, he was away from the table most of the time and he gets a hell of a kick out of sneaking drinks on the side. He thinks he's putting something over on us."

"Aren't you going to undress him?" asked Vera.

"Naw, let him sweat it out. He'll feel better in the morning."

Crolley was wearing his flying suit and GI shoes. McDevin picked his hat up from the floor, put it on the drunken navigator's head, and piled all the blankets he could find on top of him.

"I think you're mean," said Vera.

"You think *I'm* mean?" said McDevin. "You should see some of the things he's done to me."

A boy brought two more bottles of cognac and McDevin and Vera drank heartily. Dick didn't stir.

"Let's go to bed," said Vera, and she began to undress.

"You know I'm having the damnedest experiences," said McDevin. "Night before last I was sleeping with a girl in London. Today I get shot down and bail out of an airplane. And tonight I'm drunk on cognac and sleeping with an American girl in Brussels. The funny part about it is, I'm taking it in my stride. Things just move too fast for me." And he began to undress.

CROLLEY DREAMED AROUT JUNGLE HEAT AND THE SWEAT BATHS of the Elk's Club at home. Then he flitted from one smelting furnace to the next, in Gary, Indiana. After that he was running through the flames of hell and then Percy Smithsonian, his cadet colonel in navigator's school, gave him a hot-foot. During all this, Mrs. Chyb, his fifth grade teacher, was thumping him on the head with a ruler, and he was receiving the beating of his life in a sandlot game on Plum Street in Springfield. As he was methodically beating his head against a brick wall, someone on the second story poured hot water over him, and he opened his eyes. He groaned.

"I must be dead," he thought, "and I've gone to hell on top of it. No one could feel so bad and be so hot and still live."

As he regained his senses he began to grasp the situation. He knew he was in a hotel room and, taking close inventory, he realized that he was covered with numerous blankets. As he raised his head and looked around he saw a cognac bottle. It was then that he knew that his physical suffering was the result of his previous night's indulgence and a sinister prank, conceived and carried out by his erstwhile best friend, Michael Patrick McDevin. He lay motionless and planned fearful retribution. Raising his head gingerly, he saw two bodies in the twin bed beside him. This was a golden opportunity, he thought. But after consideration he decided that he was not physically up to it. He got out of bed slowly and lay for a moment on the floor. He removed his clothes, taking great care not to disturb his aching head, and crawled to the bathroom on his hands and knees. With difficulty, he pulled himself into the bathtub. With one final Herculean effort, he turned on the cold water. He screamed in agony as the icy spears from the shower struck his body.

McDevin sat up abruptly in bed, at a loss as to the source of the piercing noise. He felt Vera's warm body next to him and, with apprehension, he ran to the bathroom.

"What's your trouble, Dick? You sound like you're being tortured."

"Tortured, hell. It's worse than that. I'm being drowned and frozen to death at the same time. Turn off this water, will you? I can't move."

"Why did you turn it on, stupid?"

"Because I was burning up, that's why. Some son of a bitch put me to bed last night with my clothes on and covered me with a half a dozen blankets. I'm not mentioning any names, but his initials are Michael McDevin and I've put him at the top of my list."

McDevin began to laugh. "Vera and I almost burst a gut laughing at you last night, when you came home. Where in the hell had you been, anyhow?"

"How should I know?" answered Crolley belligerently. "The last thing I remember I was chasing some gal around a commode. Then I woke up with a hell of a hangover and soaking wet. If I'd stayed sober maybe I could have slept with Vera."

"Not a chance," said McDevin. "I got that baby sewed up. She screamed 'uncle' last night and I had to let her go to sleep."

"You bombardiers are all crooks," answered Crolley, "and without exception you are the lowest of them all."

"We'd better get dressed," said McDevin. "Maybe the limeys have a plane for us."

"Let's hope they haven't," answered Crolley. "I could never make it today."

Without comment McDevin went back to the bedroom and began to dress. Vera awoke when he was half attired and stretched her long body.

"Where are you going, darling?" she asked. "Don't tell me you were going to leave me to face the cold world alone this morning, hangover and all?"

"We're going out to the field to see if we've got wings back to Merrie Ole England," said McDevin.

"Yeah, we can't wait to get back to Piccadilly," chimed in Crolley, despite his aching head.

"Fine thing," said Vera. "What have they got in Piccadilly that I don't have right here?"

"Not a damn thing," said McDevin, "except clean clothes, my money, and a one-way ticket to the U. S. A."

"Besides that," added Crolley, "he's got a girl in Cambridge he thinks is with child."

Vera got out of bed, fluffed her hair, and walked to the bathroom. Before closing the door, she said, "Don't leave without kissing me good-by. I'll be out of here in a jiffy."

Vera returned to the bedroom, her long flowing body shimmering in the sunlight that streamed through the windows. "I've got a suggestion for you big men. I hope you don't mind taking it from a mere woman," she said, and she poured herself a drink from one of the bottles of cognac.

"Spill it," said Crolley impatiently. "We're in a hurry."

"Well," said Vera, "you don't know that they've got a plane for you, do you?"

"No," admitted McDevin.

"And you don't have any way to get out to the field," she continued.

"No," admitted McDevin again.

"Then why in the hell don't you call them on the telephone?"

"I never thought of that," said Crolley with some embarrassment. "How about getting the field for us, Vera? We can't speak this frog. When you get the base, just ask for the RAF Operations Office."

"Wait until I slip something on," she said. "I might shock some of those English lads, talking over the telephone naked."

"You're a scream," said Crolley without enthusiasm.

After a considerable harangue with the hotel clerk, telephone operators and the communications people at the airfield, Vera finally got the proper person on the other end of the line. McDevin did the talking and found out that a C-47 was expected at noon to pick them up and fly them back to England.

McDevin and Crolley were jubilant. They ate a sparse breakfast, checked out of the hotel, and bid Vera a passionate good-by. They traveled the distance to the airfield by trolley car and shank's mare.

The British were even cooler than they had been the night before. Crolley started to do bodily harm to one fellow who contemptuously remarked that the Americans would probably get a medal for bailing out. McDevin saved the day by drawing Crolley away by the arm, saying it was time to board their plane.

"What did you want to do a thing like that for? We're supposed to be allies," McDevin scolded.

"Those guys burn me up," complained Crolley. "And what makes me so damned mad is the fact that the bastard was probably right. No doubt we *will* get a medal—and we don't deserve it."

"Well, if he's right, why get all hepped-up about it?" asked McDevin with irritation.

The two boarded a waiting C-47 and sat up forward. The pilot taxied to the runway and within a matter of minutes they were airborne and on their way to the British Isles and safety.

Their aircraft was equipped with passenger seats and Crolley and McDevin leaned back, taking full advantage of being guests, for a change, instead of crew members.

"You know, I've been doing some thinking," said Mike seriously. "It's been two and a half months since we arrived overseas. We've flown eleven missions and now we'll probably be sent home. On top of that, a girl has fallen in love with me and, to make matters worse, I've slept with her. Seems just like fiction to me, the way that just a little more than two months can do so much to your life." He sighed.

"You think too much," said Crolley. "And you attach too much importance to things that don't mean a damn."

"What have I said that didn't mean a damn?" protested McDevin.

"The part about Linda," answered Crolley. "You have no indication other than her statement that she's in love with you. Hell, you've only seen her five or six times. How can she tell? And as far as her being pregnant is concerned, I explained all about the birds and bees to you on the way home from London the day before yesterday. Now why in the hell don't you just forget about it? Let's consider ourselves damn lucky. We'll be home in a month and when you see Katherine again you'll forget that you ever knew Linda."

"Are you insinuating that I may be in *love* with Linda?" asked McDevin in surprise.

"Not really," said Crolley. "It's just a sexual attraction, nothing more."

"Hell, I know that," said McDevin. "But what did you mean

by the statement that as soon as I saw Katherine again I'd forget Linda? You intimated love."

"I did no such thing. I simply meant that you're too soft-hearted a guy to hurt anybody, and you'll probably keep on worrying about whether she is in love with you, or whether she's pregnant, not because you love her, but because you feel sorry for her."

"You're a queer duck, Crolley," said McDevin. "When we're out on a party you don't have a lick of sense and I've got to lead you around by the hand. When it comes to seducing a woman you're about as subtle as the air in a pet shop. But when we talk things over and try to reason them out, you're downright sensible. I don't get it."

Crolley heaved a long sigh and came to a sudden decision. "Mike," he said sharply, "I'm going to tell you something. I'm going to tell you and then I'm going to forget it and never mention it again. Don't interrupt me. The only reason I'm saying this is because I'm your friend and I don't want to see you go to hell over a little whore. You've got a wife and baby and I hate to see you ruin their lives as well as yours, because of your blind faith in humanity and that great big heart you've got beating inside that skinny chest of yours."

He hesitated just a moment and stared at McDevin, then began again, slowly, with determination.

"Mike, do you remember that night at the Officers' Club, when you met Linda? And do you remember when I didn't come home until late the next morning and told you that I had spent the night passed out on the floor of the club annex? I lied to you. I spent it in Lavenham in Robbin's Hotel—with Linda, Mike, and she charged me five pounds. She's nothing but a whore, you damned boob. She's no better than those bitches that hang out on Piccadilly Circus.

"She doesn't work for the government. She gave up her job in a defense plant and has had her privilege to work taken away from her. Doris told me that. I'm sorry I didn't tell you before, but she made me promise I wouldn't. Besides, I thought it would make you mad.

"If she's pregnant, Mike, I'm just as much subject to blame as you, and I don't give a damn. How do you suppose she just accidentally ran into you in London? It's because she spends most

158

all of her time in those bottle clubs. Old Maury hires her just like he does the rest of them. The reason she's got an apartment in Cambridge is because she's married. Her husband's a sailor in His Majesty's Navy. That 'mother' business is just a gag. All this I got from Doris, too.

"She *is* in love with you, Mike. I know she is. She even told me she was, and I believed her. I still do. But the fact remains that she's still a common, ordinary whore, and she's taking you for a ride. Now don't say a goddamn word, because I'm going to sleep."

* * * * * *

OFFICER'S CALL WILL BE HELD ON PROMENADE DECK AFT, IM- mediately. Repeat, Officer's Call will be held on promenade deck aft, immediately," droned the ship's address system. Lieutenant Michael Patrick McDevin leaned heavily against the ship's rail- ing. The transport was just pulling away from the Liverpool docks and McDevin began to walk slowly toward the gathering crowd of officers.

"Hey, Mike!" It was Crolley.

"I've been looking all over for you—been in every latrine on the ship."

"Hi, Dick," said Mike with affection. "Don't you ever run down?"

"Hell, no," he answered gaily. "Why should I? We're going home, aren't we? Too bad Canyon and the rest of the crew aren't here."

"I'm sorry that we were so eager to get out of the Group," said McDevin sadly. "They would have had their orders in an- other week."

"I'm glad we're here and on our way," said Dick. "Don't
159

forget they'll have to go through processing at Chorley yet. Besides, I've been sweating out getting you on this boat—I've got something to tell you."

"Shoot," said McDevin.

"Mike, you remember that tale I told you when we were flying back from Brussels, that I said I wouldn't mention again?"

"Yeah," answered McDevin in wonder.

"It was a fairy tale, Mike. I *did* spend the night on the floor of the Officers' Club annex."

McDevin flushed deeply. "Goddamn you, Crolley . . ." he began.

"Don't get excited, laddie. She'll never bother you again. She thinks you're dead. I called her up and told her so the day after we got back to the Group."

"Why did you have to poke your nose into it in the first place?" said McDevin, still belligerent.

"Like I told you before," answered Crolley. "I didn't want you to ruin the lives of your family. The reason I brought it up again is to teach you a lesson, one that you needed very badly. In our business, buddy, it's love 'em and leave 'em."

THE END